VERA

Ans		M.L. 09/08 (Betty)
ASH		MLW
Bev		
C.C.		
C.P.		
Dick		
DRZ		
ECH		
ECS		Pion.P. 2/09
Gar 07/08		Q.A.
GRM 5/07 Lika		Riv
GSP		RPP
G.V.		Ross 12/08 (McGe)
Har		S.C. 11/07 (Jant
JPCP		St.A.
KEN 2/07 Srek		St.J
K.L. 3/08 (Szmiec)		St.Joa
K.M.		St.M.
L.H.		Sgt 01/07 (Long)
LO		T.H.
Lyn		TLLO
L.V. 06/08 (Json)		T.M. 10/09
McC		T.T.
McG		Ven
McQ 6/08		Vets
MIL		VP 12/06 John
Heiland 4/08		Wat
Stempien 12/08		Wed
		WIL
		W.L.

D0700554

SPECIAL MESSAGE TO READERS

This book is published under the auspices of

THE ULVERSCROFT FOUNDATION

(registered charity No. 264873 UK)

Established in 1972 to provide funds for research, diagnosis and treatment of eye diseases. Examples of contributions made are: —

A Children's Assessment Unit at Moorfield's Hospital, London.

•

Twin operating theatres at the Western Ophthalmic Hospital, London.

•

A Chair of Ophthalmology at the Royal Australian College of Ophthalmologists.

•

The Ulverscroft Children's Eye Unit at the Great Ormond Street Hospital For Sick Children, London.

You can help further the work of the Foundation by making a donation or leaving a legacy. Every contribution, no matter how small, is received with gratitude. Please write for details to:

THE ULVERSCROFT FOUNDATION,
The Green, Bradgate Road, Anstey,
Leicester LE7 7FU, England.
Telephone: (0116) 236 4325

In Australia write to:
THE ULVERSCROFT FOUNDATION,
c/o The Royal Australian and New Zealand
College of Ophthalmologists,
94-98, Chalmers Street, Surry Hills,
N.S.W. 2010, Australia

ONLY ONE CAN PLAY

Living in Barnscombe in Devon, Karen and Greg were happily married, but after a series of suspicious accidents, Karen left her husband. Who would want to harm her? Surely not Greg himself, or Mark, his partner? Or Tim, her first love, with his own life to lead? As for her sister, Jenny, men to her were just stepping-stones to success. Karen needed to leave Devon to find the answers — she might not live long enough if she stayed.

Books by Mary Landy
in the Linford Romance Library:

OCTOBER GOLD

MARY LANDY

ONLY ONE CAN PLAY

Complete and Unabridged

LINFORD
Leicester

First published in Great Britain in 1978 by
Robert Hale Limited
London

First Linford Edition
published 2006
by arrangement with
Robert Hale Limited
London

Whilst several place-names in this book are real,
all the characters are fictitious.

Copyright © 1978 by Mary Landy
All rights reserved

British Library CIP Data

Landy, Mary
    Only one can play.—Large print ed.—
Linford romance library
    1. Romantic suspense novels
    2. Large type books
    I. Title
    823.9'14 [F]

    ISBN 1–84617–495–3

Published by
F. A. Thorpe (Publishing)
Anstey, Leicestershire

Set by Words & Graphics Ltd.
Anstey, Leicestershire
Printed and bound in Great Britain by
T. J. International Ltd., Padstow, Cornwall

This book is printed on acid-free paper .

For Thea

Part One

1

Karen was twenty-eight when she parted from Greg Marshall. She left the house the day after the third attempt on her life. She reckoned it was possible she could have been mistaken about the first two. But there's nothing accidental about a length of wire fixed from wall to banister at the head of the stairs.

★   ★   ★

Karen's parents had lived devotedly together till the day they died. Karen had floated serenely up the aisle in just such a happy expectation. Then where had it gone wrong? Maybe the holiday in Austria, maybe the trouble at the office. Or was it, simply, Jenny?

★   ★   ★

It was ten-thirty on a warm morning in June when Karen closed the sky-blue front door firmly behind her and slid the key under the third flower-pot from the left outside the kitchen window. That was where Greg always looked for it if he'd lent his own to Mark. That was where he'd look when she didn't come back.

The taxi she'd ordered by telephone hadn't yet arrived. She stood with her suitcases by the front gate, seeing beyond the road and across the golf course the shimmering summer sea. The broom was coming out on the edge of the fairway: the sharp tang of seaweed came in on the breeze. Hard to leave at any time, Barnscombe and the white-painted house with the blue shutters ... Karen thought of the length of wire, coiled like a venomous snake, at the bottom of the smaller suitcase and fixed her eyes on the corner round which the taxi must come.

★ ★ ★

Breakfast hadn't been an ordeal after all. Jenny was still there and Tim, who'd stayed overnight. Fortunately Jenny had been due to leave today anyway so there was no problem about that. As for Greg . . . But she didn't want to think about Greg. Not yet. Not till she could get right away and work out the story from the beginning.

2

Karen was in her second year at RADA when she realized that talent was not enough. Silver-blonde hair, wide grey eyes, a certain cast of feature — that and a limited facility for burlesquing a character had eventually led her into the precarious world of repertory theatre. Sleazy rooms, inadequate rehearsals, tepid audiences — these she could take and even enjoy because she was young and the best was yet to come. She graduated, without recourse to the casting-couch, to the bigger companies and finally to a pre-West End tryout at Brighton. That was where she met Greg.

There was nothing romantic about their first encounter. He didn't sit in the front row of the stalls, night after night. He didn't send her flowers or hang around the stage door. He knocked her off her bicycle just outside the entrance to the West Pier.

'You great oaf!' stormed Karen. 'You ...' She looked up at him and swallowed a mouthful of the epithets an actress automatically acquires. She struggled to a sitting position.

'Let's forget the broken leg and multiple contusions,' she said with dignity. 'But you might at least have had some respect for my bike.'

Greg Marshall bent his six-foot length and put her gently on her feet. He apologized for not looking where he was going.

'All medical bills are, of course, my responsibility,' he said gravely. And added, 'When you give me the right, I'll buy a new bicycle.'

'Have you any family?' he asked her over supper at the Ship after the show.

'Only a young sister,' Karen answered blithely. 'She's no trouble.'

★   ★   ★

Brighton in April. But it was no conventional spring. Waves lashed the pier and the sea wall. Spray drifted over the promenade. Brief periods of cold sunshine were offset by biting showers.

'Brighton without visitors,' said Karen, looking at a row of Regency houses, 'is like Hedda Gabler — pared to the bone.'

'All your metaphors are theatrical ones.' Greg put his hands on her shoulders. 'Will you mind very much, giving it up?'

'It never was a career in capital letters,' Karen assured him. The twins would miss her because they'd shared the same tours for so long. And Tim, of course . . . 'I'll stay in Branscombe till you come back. And we'll be married in June.'

★　★　★

Greg had been born in Canada. His mother was dead, he also told her, but his father, who owned a sawmill, still lived in Prince George. Greg had lived with the mill till his eighteenth year. This was when he decided timber was not for him. He came to London to study journalism and decided to stay in England.

He flew back to Canada in mid-April. Just for six weeks, he said, to wind up personal affairs. Karen accepted that. The itinerant life had accustomed her to sudden departures. She didn't even question the importance of the affairs which necessitated a round trip of more than seven thousand miles.

★   ★   ★

From the beginning, it was the attraction of the unknown. Greg had never met an actress before ('What in Prince George, B.C.?') and to Karen Canada meant the Heights of Quebec and the Olympic Games. Instant awareness was the spur, lively curiosity a continued incentive. You could call it love at first sight.

'We've got all the time in the world,' said Karen as she kissed him goodbye at the airport.

Three years. And all the time in the world to regret.

3

Jenny had never minded being the plain one. She had always known she was going to be a writer. In her early teens she had sold a short story of astonishing precocity to one of the women's magazines and that had set the seal on ambition. When she looked in a mirror, she didn't see the jaw that was slightly too heavy or the hair that hung straight and lank. She only saw a portrait of the author — the one that would adorn the jacket of her first best-seller.

'What's a story in a woman's mag?' Karen, secretly impressed, had asked.

'Bloody hard work,' said Jenny. 'There's editorial slant, consumer reaction, permissive limit . . . ' She was then fifteen. 'You don't think you just sit down and whip off three thousand words and send it to any old mag and expect it to sell, do you?'

11

Jenny was twenty when Karen married Greg. Introduced to her future brother-in-law a week before the wedding, she registered him merely as typical romantic hero — tall, broad shouldered, dark hair, deep-set eyes. Probably attractive to lady lumberjacks, she decided, and shook hands politely. She now had a job as deputy features and fiction editor on a magazine called Denim and was re-polishing her potential best-seller in her free time.

Jenny made a disastrous bridesmaid. To begin with, shocking pink wasn't her colour and frills weren't her style. But the theatrical twins, April and May ('It isn't possible!' said Greg, appalled) had a majority and, what was more, were able to use the dresses so much admired in the second act of 'Pink Gin and Nausea.' That she dropped the bouquet didn't matter: the air of boredom, with which she retrieved it, did. Karen, eyes fixed ahead, didn't notice. Greg, who had happened to turn his head, registered his sister-in-law as a bad-tempered bitch.

The wedding was in Brighton, with an uncle of Karen's to give her away and Greg's partner as best man. The honeymoon was spent on the Italian Riviera.

* * *

The villa was perched on a hillside two hundred feet above the cove. There was a terrace of uneven slabs and a wooden table under an olive tree. Peaches were ripening against a stone wall, small oranges grew alongside rosemary and thyme. The evocative scent of sun-warmed fruit permeated the drowsy siesta hours. In the evenings, storms growled up the coast from Rapallo: the mornings reflected the light from the dancing sea. They made love in the cool shuttered bedroom and fell asleep to the lazy chirp of the crickets.

'It's too much too soon,' said Karen. 'This sort of happiness should be spread out over the rest of our lives.'

Greg held her close in his arms and

hoped she would never know how he had lied to her.

★ ★ ★

The first shadow — and it was no more than that — would never have appeared if Greg had done his own packing. But he'd gone into Rapallo to check on transport to Genoa airport and Karen, experienced in the routine of departure, started stacking his clothes in piles on the bed. The transistor radio must have been playing because she didn't hear his feet on the tiles of the hall or the creak of the third stair from the bottom. She was turning towards the bureau in the corner when she saw him standing in the doorway. Maybe it was the fact that the shutters were closed against the midday heat that gave a misleading impression of ... of what? Alarm? Menace? Then he moved forward and she saw that he was smiling.

'Darling, how clever of you!' His glance took in shirts, handkerchiefs,

14

socks, slacks. 'I'll do the rest of it. How about pouring us both a drink? I'll be down in a minute.'

Going downstairs, Karen wondered briefly if there was something in one of the bureau drawers he hadn't wanted her to see. Perhaps a present? She took the drinks out onto the terrace and forgot all about it.

All the way back to Devon by train, plane and car, Greg was never parted from the briefcase at his side. Business papers, he assured her.

4

The Misses Anstruther lived in a large house set back from the main street in Barnscombe. They had all been born there — in the days when there was one village store and nobody mentioned trade. Papa, who had reluctantly passed on ten years previously at the age of ninety-three, had kept his daughters in the schoolroom till the day of his death. By then it was too late for Agnes and Edith to come to terms with freedom. But Baby, now in her late fifties, had taken to emancipation with joyous abandon. Her faded hair tortured into a semblance of Hollywood curls, her mouth a scarlet bow, she lived (with certain up-to-date modifications such as vodka) in the world of the thirties in which her youth had been wasted. Miss Edith retired into stolid domesticity, Miss Agnes lived vicariously through her telescope.

'I see the elder Hobson girl has returned from her honeymoon,' announced Miss Agnes, sitting at her bedroom window one evening late in June. 'I suppose,' she added grudgingly, 'that actresses become respectable when they marry.' And after all, her father had been a Brigadier.

Baby Anstruther, hovering uncertainly in her sister's room till the doors of the Tucker's Arms down by the beach opened to her daily intake, reacted eagerly.

'Oh do let me see!' Karen Hobson was so pretty, rather like Sally Gray in 'Dangerous Moonlight.'

The white house with the blue shutters swam into focus. The front door was open. A man was unloading suitcases from the boot of a car. His face, at first in profile, turned towards the lens. Baby looked at him with interest. Cary Grant, maybe, in 'The Awful Truth'? No, someone more craggy. Bogart? Not really. The small silver clock on the chest of drawers struck the magic hour of six. Baby

17

relinquished the telescope. She'd think of the name later. Someone familiar, anyway . . .

The Salthouse had belonged to Karen since the death of her parents in an air crash six years previously. Originally two coastguard cottages, it had been converted and modernized a decade before Brigadier Hobson decided to retire while he was still young enough to bring his handicap down into single figures. The fact that his wife had recently inherited a considerable sum of money from her godfather meant that he could now devote himself to his life's ambition. He had just won the Captain's Cup, off a handicap of eight, at Barnscombe Golf Club, when he and Mary died on their way to fresh — if temporary — fields at Marbella. Pity, said the Captain, could have come down to six if he'd cured that hook.

Karen had no difficulty in letting the house, even in winter, for the first five years. Jenny was at boarding-school, and spent her holidays with Mary

Hobson's brother and his wife in Sevenoaks. Karen continued her career and visited her sister whenever the company was visiting the south coast. Tenants had been kind, the house agent was conscientious: the white walls sparkled, the blue shutters were repainted every year, the lawn behind the fuchsia hedge was smooth and even. To Karen, coming home with Greg, it seemed as if she had never been away.

The most significant thing about their second year of marriage was that Greg changed his job. The press-cutting agency which Mark Rycroft had been running for half-a-dozen years had been sold, advantageously, to a larger concern. Both men decided to sink their joint capital in book publishing. Carnlough Books in Honiton was an old-fashioned firm which had been declining over the last decade, chiefly because of the inability of the directors to come to terms with modern demands. Greg and Mark, with a controlling interest on the board, proposed to set up a department for unknown authors prepared to finance their own manuscripts. The response to advertising had been gratifying. Greg ran the business side: Mark, with a small team of readers, was in charge of selection and relations with clients.

The immediate effect, from Karen's point of view, was that Jenny came to stay at The Salthouse.

5

Mark Rycroft had been married at twenty, divorced at twenty-five. His wife had left him after a couple of years and returned to dragging her long skirts through the corridors of a provincial university. The air of cynical detachment he had cultivated hid a real talent for instant appraisal. In his job, it was invaluable. The only time it had let him down was his first meeting with his former wife.

He met Jenny Hobson on a boisterous Sunday morning in early April, nearly two years after Greg and Karen had got married.

'My sister-in-law is staying with us,' Greg had said earlier in the week. He added, 'Come to lunch on Sunday?'

'Like to,' said Mark laconically. The flat above the tobacconist's shop in Honiton was merely a place where he slept and worked. He spent a lot of time at The Salthouse.

'Is she staying long?' he asked without much interest.

'That, I'm afraid,' said Greg dryly, 'is up to her. Karen's mother made a stipulation in the will when she left her the house. 'Where you will always, should she need one, offer a home to your sister Jennifer Mary . . . ' Incidentally, bring your clubs. We might play nine holes before tea.'

The sea was far out in Cobbler's Bay as Mark drove down off the headland into the road leading to the house. A strong, south-westerly wind whisked the spume off the top of the waves. A cloud raced over the sun and a sudden squall obscured the horizon. Straight into the wind for the last six holes, thought Mark, as he skirted the fifth fairway. He wondered if Karen's sister played.

Karen herself opened the front door and kissed him lightly on the cheek. Her silver-gilt hair was drawn back and tied at the nape of her neck with a velvet bow, the same blue as her needlecord jeans.

'We're just having a drink. Tim turned up as well — do you remember him? Go on in. I'm just getting some ice.'

The rectangular sitting-room was at the back of the house with windows opening onto a walled garden. There was a fireplace at each end, relics of the coastguard cottages. The carpet was pale grey, curtains and covers sky-blue. Scarlet tulips grew in the window-boxes outside. Three people turned as he stood in the doorway. For a brief moment he wondered if they had been talking about him. That would explain the sudden silence. But not the subtle air of tension . . . Then Greg moved forward.

'Hi, there! Come on in. You remember Tim Malone? And this is Jenny.'

She was wearing jeans, not a long skirt. Her hair was cut short, with a sweep over the forehead. Her eyes were grey, not amber. But the shape of the face was Judy's. And the air of abstraction . . . Not again, vowed Mark. Never again. If he ever fell in love, it would be with someone serene and lovely. Not a half-baked student with delusions of grandeur.

'How do you do,' he said formally.

He accepted a gin-and-tonic from Greg. He took a quick sip.

'Bet you a ball you hook into the sea at the sixth,' he said.

'You're on! The tide won't be that far in.'

'You don't know how I've worked out the odds. Hullo, Tim! You playing too?'

If there had been any tension, it dissipated during lunch. Seated at the oval table in the dining-room, the atmosphere was one of easy formality. If Karen contributed little to the conversation, it was she who set the tone. Greg carved the lamb and poured the wine and followed her lead. Afterwards, Karen remembered that sparkling lunch as the last

carefree hour the five of them were
ever to spend together.

* * *

It was three o'clock before the men left
for the Golf Club. There was a flurry of
comment and suggestion as they
finished coffee and got to their feet.

'Lovely lunch, Karen. Pity we can't
just sit here and think about it.'

'Can I come and caddy?' That was
Jenny.

'Not in those heels, you can't!'

'You'll need a sweater, Tim. Have you
got one with you?'

'How about you, Karen? '

'No, thanks. I'll clear up here and
then have a walk on the beach.'

'Bet you can't make Torhead Steps
and back before tea!'

'Anyone seen my five-iron?'

'Get a move on, Jenny . . . '

'See you later . . . '

* * *

25

Someone had said that the tide wouldn't be far in. Someone had neglected to point out that there was a spring tide and a strong on-shore wind.

6

Torhead Steps was a misnomer because there was no way up the towering cliff at the far end of Cobbler's Bay. The so-called steps were a series of ledges in the red sandstone which petered out a mere thirty feet from the beach. It was a popular picnic rendezvous, being a landmark for the safe bathing of Magdalene Sands on the way to Start Point. Access from Barnscombe was around the headland from the dunes beside the golf course.

Karen skipped along the firm sand, skirting the pools left by the retreating tide. She liked having an objective for a walk, so why not win the bet? She'd forgotten who had suggested it, but the others would remember. She came to the line of jagged slabs which marked the entrance to Cobbler's Bay and made her way carefully over the rocks in her rope-soled shoes. She slipped momentarily on a piece of seaweed, then jumped down onto the beach. The wind buffeting the hood of her anorak, the familiar thunder of the waves in her ears, she walked towards Torhead. She was wondering what she was going to do about Jenny.

She reached the far end of the bay and turned to retrace her steps. It was only when a line of foam brushed against her shoe that she raised her eyes, startled. The tide, surely, should be only halfway in? What she saw brought her to an abrupt standstill. The ridge of rocks pointing the only way back to Barnscombe had disappeared.

⋆   ⋆   ⋆

'Must be the spring tide,' remarked Tim, looking across from the third tee to the breakers creaming up the beach. 'Got my driver, Jenny?'

'I'm caddying for Greg, not you!' He noted the spark in her eyes and decided to let it go. Jenny, especially with a glass or two of wine inside her, was unpredictable. He hit a long ball which caught the natural bunker in the middle of the fairway. The wind whistled through his thick dark-brown hair. He swore at the bunker.

'The meanest committee member,' agreed Greg, 'couldn't have positioned it better.'

* * *

Karen had once won the hundred yard sprint at school. Even with the handicap of the years between and the added disadvantage of crumbling Devon sand instead of smooth Berkshire turf, much of the old turn of speed sent her feet pounding towards the headland. But any hope of swimming round to Barnscombe was immediately dashed. As she watched, a wave foamed its way along the now submerged rocks, hurled itself in a smother of spray against the point and retired with a vicious backwash. Within seconds, another one came sweeping in. She turned towards the inward curve of the bay and stood looking up at the sheer rock face. The words of the notice for summer visitors, so familiar as to be disregarded, came reluctantly to her mind. 'It is necessary to study the tide before going too far east or west, as there is no way of escape up the steep cliffs.'

★ ★ ★

Jenny was surprisingly docile, thought Greg. None of those barbed little remarks about the basic futility of golf. Quite a fetching little bottom she had in those tight-cut jeans, bouncing along in front of his trolley . . .

★ ★ ★

Karen came back to the edge of the submerged reef. There was nothing else for it. It would have to be the underwater channel.

30

She hadn't used it for years, she wasn't even sure where it was, but at least it must still be there. She took off her anorak and rolled it into a ball. Then she discarded her shoes and waded into the surf.

The channel was a deep fissure which ran straight through the mass of rock separating the two bays. Karen had discovered it soon after the family arrived in Barnscombe, but only once had she inched her way along with a couple of feet of water above her head. On that day the sea had been smooth as silk and she had known that she could surface at any time. On that occasion, enjoyment had been lightly spiced with danger. This time it was a matter of survival.

★   ★   ★

Mark wiped the spray from his dark glasses and played a delicate shot to the last green. Shy with women, he was easy and relaxed on the golf course.

31

Jenny watched him. She appreciated expertise. Her eyes went beyond the green to the sea surging up to the base of the sandhills.

* * *

Karen stood in the water, fighting to keep her balance, eyes searching desperately for a known landmark. A wave, smaller than the others, retreated, and suddenly she saw it — the large flat rock on which she used to leave her towel. Now she knew where the opening was. She took a deep breath and dived.

The channel was no more than thirty inches in width. Swimming was impossible, even the dog-paddle of earlier adventures. The only way of advance was to pull herself along by means of handholes on either side. The distance was maybe only twenty yards, easy in normal conditions. But the incessant movement of the water and the ear-splitting churning of the waves just above her head made for slow progress. Her lungs were near to bursting when her groping hands encountered a solid slab directly ahead. The truth was inescapable. The exit, the only way out to Barnscombe sands, was blocked.

She didn't have to make a decision. One had to breathe. It was as simple as that. She shot to the surface. A wall of water was retreating with the speed of a mill-race. It was probably her anorak which saved her. Still with her finger through the label, as she'd dragged it through the channel, she had a split second in which to float it in front of her face as she crashed into a spike of rock standing solidly erect. Winded, bruised, soaked and shivering, she was still alive. And with time to make a lunge for dry land not ten feet away.

She was home in time for tea. Under the circumstances, she refrained from asking who had made the bet. It was enough to know that she had won it.

7

Tim Malone was very nearly a good actor. He had been an automatic choice for leading parts in the company in which he and Karen had been together and which had proved his launching pad to television success. A TV director, weekending in Bournemouth, had chanced to see the local version of 'Private Lives.' As he needed an unknown and relatively inexpensive lead for a thirteen-part series entitled 'Repertory', he signed up Tim Malone on the spot. Tim offered to Karen fame and fortune.

'You'll come to London with me, won't you? We could get married . . .'

$$\star \quad \star \quad \star$$

It was, surprisingly, Jenny who brought them together again. She was introduced to him at a party in Hampstead given by the editor of 'Denim'. Tim, now well-known in television, had been brought along by his agent.

'Hobson?' he said without much interest. 'It would be too much to expect you have a sister called Karen.'

'How did you guess? It can't be because of any resemblance.' Jenny's voice was faintly acid. She had learned, chiefly through contact with the other girls at 'Denim', that a caustic tongue can compensate for lack of the more obvious attractions. 'I'm the plain one,' she added and smiled. A smile can go a long way too if it's used sparingly. Tim Malone didn't bother to contradict her. But he decided there was more to this young sister of Karen's than he'd thought.

'You with this outfit?' he asked, offering her a cigarette.

'It pays enough to give me time off to write.'

'Novels?' Tim deliberately put off the moment of finding out what Karen was doing, where she was.

'Yes,' said Jenny briefly.

'Romantic?' Not that she looked the part but you could never tell.

Jenny was used to this question. Her anti-hero was an underprivileged footballer who lived in Nottingham.

'Realism,' she said. That put the stopper on most cocktail party conversations. 'Oh really?' they'd say and drift off. Tim didn't move.

'How's Karen?' he asked.

Jenny had never had much interest in her sister's friends. Men had appeared at Karen's side from time to time, been introduced, bought her ice-cream or — more lately — Campari and soda. Tim was different. Tim spelt success. Why on earth had Karen let him get away?

'She's in Brighton at the moment.' No need to mention Greg at this stage. After all, they weren't married yet. Let Karen be the lure.

'Why don't you come down on Saturday?' Jenny said casually. 'There's a party after the show.'

* ★ ★

The series entitled 'Repertory' rose to third place in the popularity charts. Tim played the part of a not quite first-class actor in a repertory company and had the sense not to embellish. A fine natural performance, said most of the reviewers. One carping critic suggested that maybe the lad didn't even have to try, but his was a provincial weekly which few appreciated or even read. Simon Harvard, as portrayed by Tim Malone, became a household name.

★ ★ ★

That had been more than three years ago. When the series ended, there had been offers. Many of them. Tim had unfortunately chosen to play a neurotic subaltern in a war saga and his ratings had been nil. Mis-cast had been the kindest assessment. Since then he had hovered on the fringes and at the moment had a small part in a domestic comedy at Finsbury Park.

Karen had been glad to see him again and thankful that he seemed to have rationalized their love affair. He even brought a girl to spend one summer weekend. Her hair was black and her body tanned golden-brown and her name was Marisa. She didn't speak much English but she smiled a lot and everyone liked her.

Now that Karen was married, Tim found that the rôle of family friend fitted in very well with his plans. He could afford to be patient.

8

Karen and Greg had their quarrels, the ordinary stuff of married life. In over two years, there had only been one ding-dong battle. But that one had touched a fundamental issue: Greg's obsessive love of order versus Karen's easy-going way of life.

It had been a scorching day near the end of summer. By evening bronze-tipped clouds were massing on the horizon, lividly reflected in the slow-moving sea. Greg had been working overtime on the firm's autumn budget, Karen was battling with a complicated recipe. When Greg came into the kitchen in search of beer, Karen had just knocked over a carton of yoghourt. It was the air of weary patience, as he bent to mop up the mess, that focussed her frustration. Face flushed from the heat of the stove, hair tangled, feet bare, she snatched the cloth from his hand.

'I'll do it!' she snapped.

The sauce boiled over, extinguished the gas and subsided.

'I don't mind having bacon and eggs,' said Greg unwisely. The saucepan sailed past his shoulder. Its contents streaked his favourite shirt.

'You . . . ' He caught her shoulders and shook her. 'Why can't you use a bit of method?'

'If you want everything aligned to a millimeter,' stormed Karen, 'you can go back to your bloody sawmill!'

Karen, quick-tempered, was also quick to forgive.

'Oh darling!' she said remorsefully, 'your poor shirt. I'll clean it up for you.' The dish-cloth she used had seen better days but Greg didn't complain. Thankfully, he put his arms around her.

Neither made the mistake of empty promises. Karen, who loved him, was wise enough not to change her nature for him. Greg continued to be both fascinated and irritated by the chaos in the kitchen but was honest in appreciation of the end product. Each confidently expected the other to compromise. They couldn't know then that, for one of them, it was too late to compromise.

★ ★ ★

It was just outside the kitchen door that Tim was an inadvertent eavesdropper on an early morning conversation. He had stayed overnight and wandered downstairs in search of coffee. Hand on doorknob, he heard the mention of his own name.

'Tim? He's still asleep, I think. I'll give him a shout when I've made the toast.' There was a brief clatter and the sound of Greg's voice saying something indistinguishable.

'Of course I had proposals, darling . . . ' Karen said, 'but you're the one I wanted to marry.' There was a brief pause.

'I couldn't bear the thought of losing you.' Greg's voice was muffled as if his face was against her hair. 'Would you have waited if . . . '

Tim took an involuntary step backwards and his hand rattled the doorknob. There was a sudden silence and the smell of burning toast. There was nothing for it now but to go in. Greg was putting fresh bread in the toaster. Karen was pouring out coffee.

'Don't let me interrupt this moment of togetherness,' said Tim. The tone was ironic, but just for a moment Karen thought she detected a gleam of what was surely dislike. She glanced quickly at Greg. He didn't seem to have noticed. Tim couldn't be jealous of Greg, not after all this time, could he? She hoped not. Karen was no advocate of peace at any price. If there should be differences of opinion, they were private: between herself and Greg and subsequently resolved. Any outsider causing undercurrents would not be invited again. Tim, as if sensing her thoughts, smiled at her.

'Or should I have called it meaning-ful dialogue?' he asked.

Pity, he thought later, that he hadn't heard the end of the conversation. Anything to do with Karen's marriage was worth filing away for reference.

9

The second incident had been in Austria. A holiday that promised so much and ended in near-disaster.

It was Greg who suggested going away for Christmas.

'Let's go skiing,' he said one day towards the end of a damp, misty November. 'I miss it. I used to go every winter to Jasper.'

'I did a bit when I was ten. Daddy was stationed in Germany then. They weren't real mountains, though. I'd love to go to Austria. Could we?'

Greg riffled through the batch of brochures he'd tossed onto the kitchen table.

'Hey, what was that place of Marisa's? You know, Tim's girl . . . Where did she say she lived? Dornberg, wasn't it? Let's see what the travel agents have to say about it.'

Karen remembered afterwards that Greg had broached the idea of skiing, that she had suggested Austria and he had come up with the name Dornberg. It hadn't seemed significant at the time.

Dornberg was a village nearly two thousand meters up in the Oetztal Alps. The Marshalls arrived at the end of the third week in December. It was late afternoon. Christmas trees in the windows blazed with light, throwing blue shadows on the hard-packed snow of the village street. The only sounds were the crunch of ski-boots, voices and laughter, a distant sleighbell. An onion spire was etched against the western sky.

'Austria!' sighed Karen.

'Look at all that snow!' exhulted Greg.

* * *

It was Greg who caught the first glimpse of Marisa. He was taking a breather halfway down the Red Run a couple of days after Christmas when a figure appeared at the top of the long schuss he had just negotiated. Not for nothing was this run labelled For Experts Only, he thought, as he watched the unknown skier hunch shoulders and prepare to take it straight. He himself, not yet used to the terrain, had braked three or four times during the descent and still found the speed only just controllable.

She swept past him, wearing a slim one-piece suit in dark blue. She must have been travelling at nearly seventy m.p.h. Her skis clattered on an icy bend, then she was gone.

Her hair was pushed under a woollen cap and she wore goggles. But the curve of cheek and the upturned nose were unmistakable. It must be Marisa. Greg shoved his sticks into the snow, jumped into the start and followed.

The icy bend was immediately followed by another. He rode it high, like a bobsleigh run. There was a narrow gully, then the piste widened and for a short way joined the easier Blue Run. Watching for the red arrows, he bore left again. He registered a warning notice above a steep drop and braked in time to slide round in a smooth turn before the next drop towards the village. This was sheer mindless exhileration. Momentarily he caught sight of the flying blue figure a hundred feet below. Then she disappeared again. When he finally pulled up at the cable-car station, exhausted and triumphant, she had gone.

'I thought I could ski but she's out of this world,' he told Karen later. 'I wish I could remember her surname, then we could find out where she lives. Ah well . . . Come on, honey, I'll take you down the beginners' run.'

'I'm sure they must know her at the ski school,' said Karen, swinging her skis across her shoulder. 'I think I'll have a day with them tomorrow, so I'll ask.'

'Marisa Weingartner?' The instructor had very blue eyes in a deeply-tanned face. 'Oh yes, I know her. I think she is leaving today to race at St. Anton.'

'Oh well,' said Greg, 'we may see her again before we go.'

★ ★ ★

Just before the accident, Karen thought she noticed a dark blue shape vanishing round the bend in front of her. But she could never swear it was Marisa.

★ ★ ★

The days flashed inexoraby by. You could say that most of them were the same. Coffee, hot rolls and dark cherry jam for breakfast, skiing all morning: a packed lunch on the terrace of a mountain hut, skiing all afternoon, followed by glühwein at one of the cafes in the village street. A leisurely bath preceded the aperitif hour, then dinner and later dancing in the cellar bar. Yet each day was different, depending on the weather, the texture of the snow, the people encountered in the hotel or on the slopes. Above all, performance on skis. Karen did the Blue Run with her class, Greg improved his time on the Red. Then there were two days left.

Tuesday, January the second. There'd been a heavy fall of snow overnight and it still drifted down sporadically throughout the morning. They had lunch in a hut near the top of the cable-car lines, sharing a wooden table with the usual crowd.

'I'll take you down the Blue,' Greg said as they retrieved their skis from the rack outside the door. Streamers of cloud still blew across the summit but the sky was clearing.

'I'll go on down and wait for you at the second bend. O.K?'

'O.K.,' answered Karen confidently. She watched him gather speed down the first slope and then followed, tacking from side to side with the controlled christies taught by the ski school. She reached the first bend then decided to take the next bit straight.

She didn't want Greg to think she was taking all day . . . At the end of the schuss she was going faster than she'd ever done before, too fast to think of stopping till the gradient lessened. Looking out anxiously for the next blue arrow, she swept round the corner to the left.

As soon as she saw the warning sign, she knew she'd come the wrong way. She also knew, with a flash of panic, that if she tried a christie and the edges of her skis failed to bite, she would slide over the edge. What saved her was a purely instinctive action. Keeping her skis flat, she pushed the left-hand one forward and put her weight on it. With the back ski acting as a brake in the old-fashioned Telemark her father had once taught her, she slithered to a halt against the new snow padding the wooden post. Only then did she topple over, slowly, painfully — and safely.

Greg was furious. 'Why the hell didn't you follow the blue arrow?' he shouted. He looked scared to death.

'I did!' answered Karen, wondering if she'd broken her wrist or merely sprained it. 'Help me up, please, Greg. I want to have a look at those arrows.'

She stood at the fork and looked at them. The blue pointed right, the red one left. Two painted signposts stuck into the snow. She couldn't help thinking it would have been only a matter of seconds to transpose them.

Later she realized that this premise presupposed a hand to return them to their original positions.

10

Tim turned up one day shortly after the Austrian holiday. Karen returned from a brief shopping expedition and found him on the doorstep.

'Tim, how nice!' She smiled at him. 'You can sign my plaster. No, only a sprain, ligaments and things. I hope you're admiring my expensive tan. You don't look too bad yourself.'

'Playing golf with the producer.'

'How are rehearsals going?'

'Terrible. Really gives one hope for the first night.'

Karen dumped her shopping and came back along the hall towards the sitting-room. She paused outside the door. Tim was at the far end, looking out of the window. He was wearing blue denim jeans and a dark roll-necked sweater. The thin, wiry figure, silhouetted against the dying day, reminded her of something . . . Then he moved and the thought slid away.

'How's Jenny getting on?' he asked.

Karen hesitated, her hand on the light switch. Not for the first time since the end of summer, she wished she could talk to someone about Jenny. Certainly not Greg. Not Mark either because she didn't know how deeply he'd been involved. She had known Tim for a long time. Telling him the whole story might put it into perspective. 'Jenny . . . ' she began.

Maybe it was instinct, maybe just a feeling that Tim knew exactly what she was thinking. Her finger moved, flooding the room with light.

'Jenny always falls on her feet,' she said lightly. 'Let's have a drink. And I want to hear all about the play. When do you plan to hit the West End?'

Greg came home soon afterwards and they all went down to the Tucker's Arms.

'We should have got Marisa's address from you before we went to Dornberg,'

Greg remarked as they faced into the salt-laden wind. 'Does she live in the village?'

'On the outskirts,' replied Tim. He didn't sound very interested. 'Up above the Pension Arlberg — I don't suppose you know it.' Greg went on talking about the skiing but Karen had stopped listening. She knew the Arlberg because her ski-school class had once come back that way from an off-piste excursion. Her photographic memory told her that for someone of Marisa's calibre it couldn't be more than a two-minute glide through the woods from the junction of the runs to the chalet above the Pension. But why should Marisa, who had stayed with them, whom they had liked, play such a foolish practical joke? Marisa who of all people would know the dangers. It didn't make sense.

Next day Tim's casual 'How's Jenny?' kept returning to mind. Karen suddenly decided she'd got to talk to someone. That was when she remembered the twins, wintering in repertory at Torquay. Who better? They knew all the protagonists, were entirely unprejudiced and would keep their mouths shut on confidences.

They met outside the Theatre Royal. Karen, who got there in time for the end of rehearsal exodus, stood outside and pulled up the fur-lined hood of her red tweed coat. So many theatres like this one — in Bath and Bridlington, Bournemouth and Berwick — she'd inspected like this, evaluating the atmosphere, imagining the audience. Did she miss the life? Of course. But she'd never swop the substance for the dream.

They came out together, April Jenkins and May Mulcahy (May having recently married the assistant stage manager), identical in tartan trews and yellow jackets, brown-haired and pug-nosed. Mrs Jenkins' little daughters had progressed in twenty years from juvenile leads to character parts without catching the eye of a single talent scout.

Indispensible as the props, they never gave an indifferent performance.

'Karen!' They swooped on her. 'Don't you look gorgeous! Let's go to the Green Man, it's always empty at this hour.'

'I didn't know what she was up to at the beginning,' said Karen ten minutes later, 'though heaven knows I should have guessed.' She lit a cigarette and started again. 'Jenny's ambition is to write a best-seller. It's only in the last year or so that she has faced the unpalatable truth that step number one is to get your masterpiece published. Oh I probably thought she'd be interested in getting Mark's opinion on the manuscript, but . . . '

'But the upshot was that she wanted Mark to approve it and Greg to print it?' suggested April.

'And have it all for free?' hazarded May.

Karen nodded. You didn't have to spell things out to the twins. 'She came to stay last April. You two haven't seen

Jenny since the wedding so I'd better explain that she's changed quite a lot. She can't do much about the shape of her face but she'd had her hair cut and conditioned and swept across her forehead and she's really got quite a good figure which she emphasizes . . . ' Karen's voice died away. She covered the cadence by taking a swig from her glass. There was one episode she'd got to talk about, bring into the open. But not now. Not yet.

'Did she try to seduce Mark?' asked April, finishing her brandy-dry.

'No. At least, I don't think so. She was rather more subtle. It's my opinion that she'd found out what Mark's ex-wife was like and played up a certain resemblance. She'd done her home-work, I'll grant her that.'

When she'd refilled the glasses, Karen come back to the quiet corner at the dark end of the saloon bar. One or two regulars had drifted in but they were out of ear-shot.

'What was she like when you were

children?' April asked. Karen thought back over the years: the brief-seeming periods with her parents in England, flying out for school holidays to Cyprus, Hong Kong, Germany.

'She was much younger. I think I was chiefly grateful that she didn't want to tag along. When she was older, she was always scribbling in corners. We weren't a demonstrative family.' No — but Karen knew she had been her father's favourite. Had Jenny minded? 'As I remember it, her chief reaction later was mild contempt. She knew that the only thing I could do with any success was interpreting other people's ideas.'

'Ambitious, ruthless . . . ' said May . . . 'and presumably imaginative?'

'Oh yes. It was a well-planned campaign. She found out that Mark's wife left him, not the other way around, not by mutual consent. She may even have gone to see the girl. Anyway, she assumed that Mark still had some feeling left for Judy and played up the resemblance. Knowing Jenny — or at least being familiar with Jenny's mannerisms — I could see what she was doing. But I thought she was wasting her time so I ignored it.'

The twins sat leaning forward, elbows on the table. 'What happened next?' they asked simultaneously.

'Mark read the novel.' Karen paused and finished her drink. 'Where Jenny made a mistake was in thinking that personal considerations would affect his professional judgment.'

'So he didn't like it?'

'On the contrary, he thought it showed a lot of promise. He was optimistic. And then something went wrong. They must have had a monumental row because Mark stopped coming to the house.'

Karen had missed Mark. She had realized how much she'd come to rely on his steadfast support and easy companionship. She had tackled Jenny and been told, with hostility, that she was imagining things.

'Nothing more happened for a bit.

Until . . . ' No, the words refused to come out. Karen knew now that she could never tell a soul what she had seen that afternoon at the beginning of September. She got abruptly to her feet.

'Thanks for listening,' she said hastily, 'but I must go. It's nearly time for my bus.' It had been a mistake to make the journey. Talking had only aggravated the feeling of moving in a mist. Maybe she *was* imagining things.

After she'd gone, the twins sat in silence. There wasn't any point, was there, in making things worse. It had been sometime in early December that they'd seen Jenny in Exeter. The car in front of them had halted at the traffic lights near the Imperial Hotel. Jenny had been in the passenger seat, turning her head to speak to the man beside her. They could have sworn that the driver was Greg Marshall.

11

The Torhead Steps episode had been in April. A couple of days afterwards, out of curiosity, she had gone back to the ridge of rocks and discovered the slab which now blocked the Barnscombe end of the channel. A curtain of seaweed masked the boulder. It was only recently, when thinking of the near-accident at Dornberg, that an elusive memory had swum into focus. There was something about that sea-weed that had looked . . . had looked arranged. Like the arrows on the piste? No, it had got to be coincidence.

One morning in February, Karen awoke with Greg's head on her shoulder and her mind miraculously clear. She would sort things out with Mark, get in touch with Jenny, put everything on a realistic basis. She even felt strong enough to face the truth about Greg. At least she'd had the sense not to make a scene, not to dissolve into the hysterics which could have torn apart the fabric of their marriage. The important thing was that they were still together.

*　*　*

The next event was the Anstruther sherry party. The idea of such an undertaking had been quite fortuitous. It was a misty February day. Vision was restricted to fifty yards.

'Balls!' said Miss Agnes, discarding the telescope. Miss Edith, her mind on the day's menus, looked up expectantly.

'You'd like meat . . . ?'

'No, dear. It's a swear-word. I heard Nancy using it yesterday. I can't say it's very satisfying. It doesn't even specify what sort . . . '

'We've never been to a ball,' said Edith suddenly. She sat in the upright chair, an apron over her second-best tweed skirt, cardigan buttoned up to high-necked blouse, Edith Anstruther who had never been alone with a man in her life. For a moment the eager girl who might-have-been looked out of the placid middle-aged face. An idea stirred in the depths of a mind normally stimulated only by esoteric recipes in the home help's discarded magazines.

'Let's have a party!' she said breathlessly.

Greg and Karen received an invitation in Miss Agnes's precise copperplate. There was a postscript: 'Please bring your partner, Mr Rycroft, and Miss Jenny Hobson if she is staying with you.'

'What do you think?' Greg looked at it doubtfully. For some reason, Baby Anstruther made him feel uneasy.

'Let's go,' said Karen. 'It might be fun, Baby was once madly in love with my father. He reminded her of Ronald Colman in Bengal Lancer.' It would be a fine excuse for reconciliation all round, she thought. Mark would accept out of courtesy. Jenny would probably see it as copy.

Realizing that anticipation might well be the better part, the sisters sent out the invitations a fortnight in advance and did some systematic planning. Each had a part to do, each a motive. Agnes saw it as the consolidation in society of Barnscombe's oldest family. Edith sensibly buried the idea of a magic new world but couldn't help hoping they'd be asked out in future to something more exciting than tea. Baby Anstruther merely saw it as an excuse for unlimited booze.

The choice of sherry was wisely left to a wine merchant in Honiton recommended by their solicitor. They borrowed a neighbour's gardener to move all the heavy Victorian furniture out of the drawing-room, washed and polished Papa's precious Waterford glass and prepared trayfuls of tiny vol-au-vent cases to bake in the old-fashioned Aga.

Unexpectedly, the party was an

uproarious success. This was partly due to the younger generation who took it as a gallant gesture and reacted accordingly, and partly to their hostesses, unfeigned enjoyment of a novel experience. Agnes, resplendent in black taffeta, and Edith, flushed and excited in unsuitable flowered chiffon, pressed excellent sherry and feathery canapés on their guests and flitted happily from group to group. Baby made an entrance as Rita Hayworth and retired to a corner with a bottle and the local librarian.

'She must have noticed the resemblance to Edward G. Robinson,' murmured Mark at Karen's shoulder.

Mark fitted in as if he'd never been absent, as if there'd never been a Jenny to disrupt his life, and Karen was so glad to see him she asked no questions. But she kept watching the door, half-hoping Jenny wouldn't come, obscurely uneasy when she didn't. She had written to her sister c/o Denim, sending on the invitation, telling her to come straight to Barnscombe House if she was late, saying she'd be welcome to stay the night at The Salthouse. There had been no reply, but there was nothing unusual in that. Jenny never wrote if she could telephone. And when she forgot that, she just turned up.

Karen glanced at her watch and looked around for Greg. There was no sign of him. Maybe he'd gone out to the kitchen to open a bottle or carry a tray . . . Greg was unfailingly kind to old ladies. A few minutes later, she saw him at the other side of the room. He was talking to a red-haired girl in a bottle green velvet suit. Attractive, registered Karen. Familiar, somehow. The girl turned and made her leisurely way towards the door. Of course, Margo Peters, the fashion editor of 'Denim' who spent most weekends at Torbay.

'Margo! How are you? I was expecting Jenny here tonight. Did she say anything to you?'

'Jenny?' Margo looked surprised.

'She isn't with 'Demin' any more.'

'But she said she was going back when she left Barnscombe in September.'

Margo's eyes suggested that September was a long time ago. Karen felt suddenly conscience-stricken. However angry she had been — and justifiably, said her brain — there was no excuse for letting the months slip by without at least finding out where her sister was. Unease deepened into something like panic.

'Margo — could you find out if she left an address? I'll phone you first thing in the morning.'

Greg was philosophical when she told him.

'Don't worry. She's probably just being temperamental. You know Jenny!' I don't, thought Karen unhappily, I never have.

Jenny's only forwarding address was the flat she had shared with two other girls in Holland Park. They reported that she had returned one evening the previous September, packed up and departed, hinting at some fabulous job in the West Country. They had never seen — or heard from — her since.

'Shouldn't we inform the police?' Karen asked despairingly.

'No,' said Greg decisively. 'She must have some good reason for staying away. She certainly wouldn't thank you for having her listed as a missing person.' But his eyes were thoughtful.

A week later a message appeared in the personal column of a popular newspaper, a paper Karen never read. 'JENNY. Come back. M.'

12

It had been early September, the end of the long hot summer. Jenny had been at The Salthouse nearly five months. Greg said that negotiations were going on, but no settlement had been reached about the publication of her book. Jenny said a new job was waiting for her at 'Denim' in the autumn. She didn't specify the date.

Karen knew the exact date of the episode which inevitably changed her relationship with Greg. In the long run maybe a measure of maturity was gained but, after September the second of that year, spontaneity was lost for ever.

Thursday afternoons, Karen worked as voluntary secretary for the Barnscombe Arts Society. The work was mostly clerical, sometimes advisory, always entertaining. It was one way of keeping in touch with theatrical events, and she enjoyed the leisurely, gossipy sessions. This particular day she had reached the large first-floor room leased by the public library to find that long-over-due decorators had just moved in. She did her share of dismantling. Then she went home.

That Greg would be home early from the office that day, she had momentarily forgotten. She entered by the front gate and went on round to the back of the house to pick roses for the dining-room table. Her feet made no sound on the close-cut turf. She had just reached the shade of the copper beach when she saw them. They were in the sitting-room, Greg with his back to the window. He was in shirt sleeves, his blue and white striped shirt. Jenny was standing close, looking up at him. They weren't speaking. They hardly seemed to be breathing. Then Jenny raised her hands and, with her eyes still fixed on Greg's face, slowly started to undo the buttons down the front of her green cotton dress.

Karen realized afterwards that there had been two other courses of action she could have taken. One was direct confrontation. The other, the diplomatic way, was to enter the house, being careful to slam the front door. Karen turned, unseen, and walked away. She knew only that she could not bear to witness the triumph on Jenny's face, the guilt on Greg's. In the late afternoon she found herself at the far end of Magdalene Sands. She was still shivering.

There were guests to dinner that night. The party, she was told afterwards, was a great success.

Karen had waited ten days before delivering an ultimatum. Ten days in which her self-control was taxed to the limit. There was no overt sign that Jenny and Greg were lovers. They didn't even make the mistake of avoiding each other. There was only a picture indelibly printed on her mind.

When she finally attacked, she made

71

sure that a trivial incident was the apparent cause of the quarrel. Jenny inadvertently smashed a cherished Meissen plate. Karen, pent-up emotion at last finding an outlet, blazed into action.

'You needn't think,' was her final thrust, 'that under the terms of the will you can make your home here as long as you like. The words 'within reason' were implied.'

★ ★ ★

Jenny reappeared, not long after the sherry party. She came back on a day of springtime promise.

Karen was busy in the garden, hoeing round the daffodil spears, when she heard the click of the gate. Shading her eyes against the morning sun, she saw her sister standing on the lawn. Jenny was looking up at the bedroom windows. There was something different about her and it wasn't just that she had started to grow her hair again.

'I haven't come to stay,' she said quickly. She carried only a shoulder bag, dark brown suede like her jacket. Her eyes were hidden behind outsize tinted glasses. Karen, torn between anger and relief, looked at her helplessly. Her first impulse, to welcome her sister with uncalculating affection, shrivelled and died.

'Where on earth have you been?' Even to her own ears, her voice had an accusing note.

'You asked me to leave — remember?' said Jenny.

It all seemed a long time ago. Karen felt her bitterness evaporate. Whatever had happened, it was all over now.

'Jenny,' she said gently, 'at least come in for a cup of coffee or a drink. I won't ask you again where you've been. All I want to know is where I can get in touch with you in the future.'

There seemed to be a response in the face so effectively guarded by the outsize dark glasses. Later Karen wondered if the smile had been genuine. Had she imagined that the expression had been one of quiet triumph?

13

The trouble in the office blew up early in June. It began with a casual visit to Carnlough Books.

'Costs going up all the time,' complained Greg.

'Materials, production, staff . . . ' agreed Mark.

'What does it actually cost to turn out a hardback?' asked Karen, who had dropped in to return a manuscript of theatrical reminiscences Mark had asked her to read.

'Obviously it varies,' answered Greg. 'Number of pages, type of paper, binding, jacket . . . '

'Well, what do you require an aspiring author to contribute?'

'For a novel of fifty thousand words, we'd bind a minimum of two hundred copies at the outset and promise an initial edition of up to two thousand:

for that we'd ask a contribution of about eight hundred pounds.' Karen whistled. 'As much as that?'

'The work of an unknown author has no predictable commercial value. Also there's . . . '

Karen cut through the sales talk with what was, in her opinion, the obvious question.

'Where on earth is Jenny going to find that sort of money?'

There was a moment's stunned silence. A typewriter clattered in the next office. Mark's head jerked up from the figures he was studying.

'From the estate, of course,' said Greg slowly. Karen stared at him.

'You mean my estate?'

'I thought Jenny said . . . ' Mark stopped suddenly.

'Surely some of it belongs to her?' That was Greg.

'The house and the money were left to me,' said Karen positively. 'There's the upkeep, as you know. A sum was also put aside for Jenny's education.

That was all used — in fact overdrawn, because Jenny managed to include that writer's course. If she were in real need, that would be different.'

'I'm afraid we'll have to ask you for that eight hundred pounds, Karen.'

'I'm sorry, Greg, but the answer is no.'

Half an hour later, they were back to where they'd started.

'Why didn't you ask me before you began printing?'

'Naturally, we assumed . . . '

'That Jenny had her own money. Did she tell you that?'

'Not in so many words.'

'I see.' No need to question Jenny's mastery of the subtle inference, the half-promise.

'It's not as if you can't afford it, honey.'

'That's not the point. If Jenny had asked me . . . '

'Would you have given it to her?' Mark asked.

'Probably not,' Karen said honestly,

'but at least I'd have had a choice.'

Together they were a formidable combination, Greg and Mark, intent on wearing her down. The next angle was the personal one.

'She really has worked on this book, you know. This is her big chance.' There were various other character references, ending with the expected 'After all, she is your sister!'

Karen looked from one to the other. She wondered if they really needed the money or if it was a matter of principle, the fulfilling of an obligation. If the former, and she'd been asked under any other circumstances to help, she'd have done so gladly. But she was damned if she'd be conned out of part of her inheritance — and that's what it amounted to. She got to her feet.

'I'm sorry,' she said again. 'But I'm not going to change my mind.'

Greg didn't come home for dinner. He still hadn't returned when Karen went to bed. The church clock chimed the hours. Finally she took a sleeping pill. Towards dawn, she thought she heard him moving about the dressing-room. When she was fully awake, he had gone.

Maybe it was the unexpected tax rebate, maybe Greg got round to admitting that Karen's attitude had a certain logic. Whatever the reason, life returned to normal. On the morning of Saturday, June the nineteenth, the sea reflected the Mediterranean blue of the sky, the roses were blooming and Karen was singing in the kitchen.

That was the day Jenny Hobson came to the Salthouse for the last time.

Part Two

GREG

1

It was ten-thirty on a warm morning in June when Karen closed the sky-blue front door firmly behind her and slid the key under the third flower-pot from the left outside the kitchen window . . .

★   ★   ★

It was a fast train to London. Karen sat in an empty compartment, her suitcases on the rack above her head. She had, at this stage, no idea where she would go or what she would do. She only knew that she had to get away.

Paddington Station was the first reminder of what she had left behind. Picking her way through the crowds in the cavernous echoing terminus, she stopped for a moment beside a queue of people inching their way towards a barrier. 'The train now standing at platform five,' a genteel voice informed her, 'is the one-fifteen for Plymouth, calling at Barnscombe, Torbay and . . . ' Karen picked up her cases and pushed her way blindly out of the station. When a taxi drew up, she said Chelsea because it was the first district to come into her mind. When she asked the driver if he knew of accommodation to rent, he took her to Oakley Street.

In the lonely days ahead, Oakley Street was to become a refuge, almost a home. On a grey London afternoon, Karen's impression was of an uncompromising Victorian house in an overall shade of dark mustard. Barnscombe had never seemed so far away. She had never needed Greg as much as at this very minute. If the taxi hadn't been re-occupied the minute she set foot on the pavement, she might have capitulated even then.

It was a good-sized bed-sitting-room with curtained off kitchen and shower. Karen methodically unpacked the clothes she had snatched from her wardrobe that morning. When she came to the coil of wire, she knelt and looked at it. She felt again the cold steel against her ankle as she stood at the top of the stairs in the early hours, wondering if Jenny had forgotten her key . . . She left it where it was and snapped the locks.

She went down into the hall and opened the front door. Some sort of action was imperative. Yet, once out in the street, the sense of urgency that had kept her going for the last twelve hours seemed to have deserted her. She walked down to the Embankment and stood with her elbows on the wall, looking down at the gently flowing river.

★   ★   ★

Lying sleepless beside Greg in the hours before dawn, fear had gradually hardened into suspicion. It had been born of the horrified realization that she was as alone as she had been when she stood with her hand on the banister, as alone as she would have been plunging head-first down the steep flight of stairs to the stone flags below. The first instinctive reaction, to run to her husband, to rouse the household, to release the tension and shock, had been instantly smothered by the new-found knowledge that there was no-one she could trust. Not even Greg. Least of all Greg. And that was the greatest shock of all. Because she had to admit that he alone had been on the spot of each of what now appeared to be three attempts on her life.

The decision to get right away had stiffened her resolution and sharpened her perceptions. The questions crowded in. For instance, had Greg really been asleep when she slid, shaking, back into bed? The moment she woke her sister next morning, was Jenny's normality overdone? Why was Tim so silent? She would never find the answers if she stayed in Barnscombe. For one thing, she might not have the time.

Any investigation would have to start
with Greg, a man she now felt she
didn't know, had never known. Short of
flying to Canada, she didn't have an
idea where to begin. Flying to Canada
. . . Greg's flight to Canada before they
were married. That could probably be
verified. If they kept records that far
back, it could be proved that Greg had
flown to Prince George, British Colum-
bia, in April nineteen seventy-three.
That at least would be a starting point.

The girl at Air Canada had short fair
hair and honey-coloured eyes. Mid-
afternoon on a Monday in June was a
slack time at the long polished counter
and she was glad to have something to
do to take her mind off the new hostess
up there in the sky with Harry. Pilots
said they never had time for air
hostesses but she knew better. She'd
been one herself.

'Three years ago?' she said. 'What
was the exact date?'

'Thursday, April the 17th,' Karen answered promptly. There hadn't been a matinée that day so she'd gone to Heathrow with Greg, sitting arm in arm in the cab all the way out from Victoria station.

'You wouldn't remember the flight number, I suppose?'

'As a matter of fact, I do, because it was the date of Trafagar. It was AC 1805, London to Edmonton.'

'I'll phone through to Records,' the girl began. 'Hey — wait a minute. I was on that route myself. April the seventeenth?' That was just after she'd noticed Harry for the first time. 'That wasn't long before Easter, was it?'

'That's right. You must have seen him!' Karen leant forward eagerly. 'Tall, dark hair, wearing a grey suit with a thin dark red stripe . . . '

Gone was the nightmare, gone the fears and suspicions. She was Karen Hobson, aged twenty-five, in love, planning to go home after Easter to prepare for her wedding.

The expression in the eyes of the girl opposite her brought her abruptly back to the present. She was Karen Marshall, past her twenty-eighth birthday, investigating the past of a husband who was a stranger.

'I wasn't flying that day. None of us were. You see, there was a strike of ground crew all over Canada. None of our planes took off for nearly ten days.'

2

Further enquiries merely confirmed the hypothesis that Gregory John Marshall had never crossed the Atlantic — at least not before the end of April, when flights were resumed. The strike had started on the fifteenth. Intending passengers had all been notified. Some of them had tried to fly to America but seats had all been booked so soon before Easter.

The inescapable conclusion was that Greg had deliberately misled her. She remembered, unwillingly, how soon after arrival at Heathrow that day — when she had insisted on coming to see him off — he had commandeered a taxi and sent her back to London en route for Brighton.

'You don't want to be rushing for the evening performance,' he had said. How considerate he was, she had thought gratefully, lovingly.

'Besides,' he had added, 'life's too short to waste on departure lounge inanities.' So she had kissed him good-bye and got into the taxi and directed the driver to Victoria. Greg had waved and turned away.

Eating a belated sandwich in a coffee bar off Piccadilly, Karen's photographic memory — boon to an actress — took over. The taxi had come to a sudden stop because of another one making a forbidden U turn. She had craned her neck out of the open window, hoping to catch a last glimpse. Greg was walking away — but not back towards the main hall. A tiny picture swam before Karen's eyes. She dropped the sandwich and finished her coffee in a gulp. What she had seen was Greg going through an opening on the right. That was all she had had time to see. But somehow she knew that it didn't lead back to the appropriate point of departure. She was suddenly convinced that whether Greg had later flown to

Canada or not, he had booked a seat for an entirely different flight on Thursday, April the seventeenth, nineteen seventy-three. There was only one way to enlarge the picture.

Driving out to London Airport, she steeled herself against failure by imagining the various innocuous places for which he could have been heading when he disappeared from view that day. A bar, the loo, the duty-free? Left luggage office, deposit boxes? If any of these conjectures was the right one, she was wasting her time.

It was after five o'clock when she reached her destination. She got out at Departures and looked around her. Yes, about twenty yards to the left was the spot where Greg had put her into the taxi. That was where he had been standing when it pulled away. And when she'd looked back from another twenty or thirty yards on, he had been walking towards an opening on the right. Karen followed the three-year-old footsteps. She turned through the glass doors and found herself in what looked like an annexe to the main hall. It contained two check-in points. One was Swissair and the other Aer Lingus. If her theory was right, it had to be Switzerland or Ireland. Which?

★　★　★

Karen stood just inside the doors and watched the passengers weigh in for a flight to Zurich at 17.56. The other check-in was at the moment unattended. She strolled over and picked up a timetable. There was one way in which she could tilt the balance. Greg would not have wanted to hang around at the airport. They had arrived in good time for the scheduled Air Canada flight he had told her was due to take off at 14.30 that Thursday. Therefore it was reasonable to assume that the plane he actually intended to board was due to leave at approximately the same time. Schedules, of course, might have altered in the interim but mostly, for the sake of convenience, they remained the same. Karen studied the Aer Lingus timetable. She felt no surprise when her eyes picked out the first afternoon flight from London to Dublin every Thursday: 14.14.

Dutifully she checked with Swissair. There was a flight to Basle at 13.45 and one to Geneva at 15.30: the first was too early while the second would have entailed hanging around for a good hour and a half. Karen turned away and made for the airline offices situated in a block at the back of the main building. At the Aer Lingus office she had her first piece of luck.

There was a black-haired young man with blue eyes at the enquiry desk. A discreet placard announced that his name was Sean O'Hara. He viewed her approach with approval. A doll if ever there was one. When he was promoted to working at the check-in he'd probably see plenty like her, but sitting where he was they were as scarce as Orangemen in the Vatican.

'Can I help you?' he asked eagerly. Karen looked at him and discarded the speech she'd prepared for the kind of official she'd expected.

'I don't know if I should be taking up your time,' she said and smiled at him, 'but it's to do with a bet.'

'Gamblers to the last breath,' the youngest of the O'Hara clan assured her.

'Well, it's like this. My husband claims he's got a phenomenal memory, so I bet him ten pounds he couldn't remember what he was doing on Thursday, April the seventeenth, nineteen seventy-three. And he said he went to Dublin that day on the two-fourteen flight from London Airport. Naturally, I didn't believe him . . . But would you have records going that far back?' she ended doubtfully.

'Oh yes, the passenger lists are filed away. Because of the Trouble, you know. He wouldn't be an IRA sympathizer, would he?'

'Oh no, he's a Canadian.' She hoped

it sounded logical. Apparently it did.

I'll do what I can,' promised Sean O'Hara. 'But it'll have to wait till I go up to head office. Maybe tomorrow or the next day.' He picked up a pencil. 'Where can I get in touch with you?' Not that there was much hope with a husband around but you never knew.

'I'll give you a ring,' said Karen hastily. 'I'm not sure where I'll be staying. The day after tomorrow? And thank you so much.'

Impatient of delay, she phoned the Aer Lingus number the following morning.

'Sorry, no Marshall at all that day. Does that mean you'll win the ten pounds?' The pride of the successful punter was barely suppressed.

'The . . . ? Oh that . . . ' Karen paused, thinking hard. She'd been so sure she was on to something. If this lead petered out, where did she go from here? In her mind she saw Greg's suitcases, G.M. embossed on leather.

'I suppose you didn't notice if there

was anyone with the same initials?' she asked without much hope. There was a rustle of paper at the other end.

'Well, I did make a note of the names . . . ' in the tone of one to whom aliases were an everyday occurrence. 'Would Gavin McGill be of any use?'

3

Reaction set in that evening. Opening a can of beans to heat up in the tiny alcove, Karen thought longingly of the big square kitchen at The Salthouse. Would Greg be cooking for himself? Did he know where she'd put his clean shirts? Was he trying to find her?

On impulse she went down to the public box in the hall and dialled the number in Torquay the twins had given her, the number which was written in the green leather book beside the telephone at The Salthouse, the first number a frantic husband would try. An innocent husband . . .

It was thinking of the green leather book that reminded her of the time Greg had talked in his sleep about Ireland. He'd once been there on holiday, he told her. There might be a link, tenuous as it seemed.

Two minutes later she replaced the receiver. The next day she flew to Dublin.

A fine rain was falling from a misty sky. The grass was magically green. The evocative smell of peat smoke drifted across from the farmhouse beyond the perimeter fence. Karen stood on the tarmac and wondered why she'd never been to Ireland before. Greg had never told her . . . Greg. Had he stood here like this, sniffing at the soft air? She sighed, picked up her lightweight bag and followed the green-uniformed hostess into the airport building. Sitting in the bus on the ten-mile ride from Collinstown into the city, her thoughts returned to the apparently insoluble problem which had nagged at her all the way over in the plane. How did she pick up the trail? Where did she even start?

Well, to begin with she had to convince herself that her assumptions so far had been the right ones. If she wasn't going to be singleminded about this mission, she might as well go back on the next flight. If she could only find a clue, however slender, she had the time and the patience and the resources to follow it up.

At the air terminal she asked for hotel recommendations and was directed to the Gresham in O'Connell Street. On impulse she asked if that was the one to which strangers were always sent.

'Not at all. Depends on the season and the bookings. Horse Show Week, now, there wouldn't be a bed available this side of Dun Laoghaire. If you'd rather have somewhere quieter, maybe you'd like the Shelbourne?'

'Would it have been the same hotels three years ago?' Karen asked.

'Sure, nothing changes much here. Have a nice holiday, now.'

Because it was first on the list, she went to the Gresham. That, she imagined, was what nine people out of ten would do, especially if they were over on business or with a specific purpose in mind. They wouldn't bother to look around for somewhere quieter, would they?

She produced her passport as she signed the register.

'Never used to ask for these,' apologized the receptionist. 'It was easy come easy go, ye know?'

It was the passport business that convinced Karen it was Gavin McGill, not Greg Marshall, whose trail she was following in Ireland. If he'd travelled as McGill, presumably he'd gone on using that name. He'd hardly have been foolish enough to carry two passports. That is, if he had two passports. Surprised, she realized that she had never seen even one. When they went to Italy and Austria, Greg had appropriated hers and dealt with all the incidentals of European travel. At home, presumably he'd kept it locked in his desk. She'd never thought of looking for it anyway. She had never invaded his privacy. Except ... A half-forgotten memory began to take shape. It was their last morning at

Rapallo and she'd been doing the packing. Greg had returned, moving swiftly and silently up the stairs, just as she was about to open the bureau where he kept his papers. Had she imagined the sudden atmosphere of menace? Maybe not. It could be that the passport was the clue she had been seeking.

Resisting the temptation offered by the register, Karen followed the porter up to her room. The book she had just signed was designed for the first half of nineteen seventy-six only, as far as she could make out. To locate the volume covering April seventy-three, she would have to approach the manager. And why should he agree to let her study his registers? She had no official standing. Even if she found the name McGill, she argued, it wouldn't get her any further to know that he had stayed at this hotel. No — it was where he'd gone from his hotel that was important.

⋆　⋆　⋆

Another town, another embankment. Karen stood on the quay and looked across the still blue-grey water of the Liffey at the white pillared Custom House. The sky had the opalescence of a Canaletto.

'I stood in Venice,' quoted a voice just behind her.

That was how she met Michael Adair. His hair was sandy, thick and straight, swept across his forehead. His face was wedge-shaped with a wide mouth. He wore natural corduroy jeans belted over slim hips and a checked shirt. He might have been thirty-five, maybe slightly older.

'When the moon shone, we did not see the candle.' The words came to her without thinking. Once learnt, never forgotten.

'I think I prefer Byron.' He looked at her with interest. 'You know Venice?'

'Only as Nerissa in rep. My best performance was at Southend-on-Sea.'

'Acclaimed, I trust?'

'The winkle-pickers liked my hair.'

101

'So do I. Will you have a drink with me? My name's Mike.'

It was just off Grafton Street. It looked like any other pub to Karen.

'You mean you've heard of Davy Byrne's?' asked Mike incredulously. Karen looked around. A seedy character in an ancient black bowler reverently invoked his deity. Four Guinness drinkers abandoned their tankards. A poet stopped disclaiming in mid-sentence.

'Blondes aren't all that common in Ireland,' explained Mike. 'Especially,' he added, 'blonde actresses who have the nerve to play in Shakespeare at Southend-on-Sea.' He found her a seat. 'What will you drink? It doesn't have to be Guinness or even John Jameson. The stockbroker belt introduced gin and tonic and it's catching on fast.' He went over to the bar.

'Now,' he said, bringing over the drinks, 'what are you doing in Dublin? Not a tourist. Tourists don't loiter by the Liffey when they could be brushing up their culture with the Book of Kells. Visiting relations? At a guess, that's unlikely. You haven't got relations in this country, have you? Not with as English an accent as ever I heard. Business trip with husband? No? Business trip without husband?' He studied her. The blue sprigged cotton suit was expensive. So were the shoes. Flyaway silk scarf at neck. Shining hair touching her shoulders. Davy Byrne's hadn't seen anything like this in all the years he'd been coming in. The Guinness drinkers in the corner, to a man, watched her with fascinated eyes.

'I'm naturally curious,' he reassured her. He looked around. 'Too many people in here,' he said abruptly. 'Let's walk.'

Down Grafton Street, past Trinity, into O'Connell Street. They were nearly at the door of the Gresham when Karen made up her mind.

'I need some help,' she said.

'McGill?' queried Mike. 'Not a particularly common name in the

103

South.' They were back on the quay, sitting on a bench overlooking the water. Karen had given him a brief outline of her years with Greg: sketching in Jenny, Mark and Tim, omitting only Greg and Jenny together.

'So you reckon he came over here because he wanted to settle some affair or other before he married you? Have you ever thought of another woman? Even — a wife?'

*   *   *

Karen stared at him with wide grey eyes. Somehow she wasn't as surprised as she would have been six months ago. Even a week ago. These last few days on her own had resuscitated some of the sturdy self-reliance of her years in the theatre.

'If so, I hope he remembered to get a divorce,' she said dryly. 'Is there a Somerset House here?'

'Sure, the Public Records Office. It's at the Four Courts, just along the quays. It'll be closed now, though. Have dinner with me. Then I'll go along first thing in the morning. No — I'll go, not you. You should be safe enough this side of the water, but I aim to keep it that way.'

He came to the hotel while she was finishing breakfast.

'Nothing relevant for Marshall. But there is a Gavin McGill, born near here, married a Dublin girl, Eileen O'Rorke from Leeson Park; he seems to be the right age to fit in with your theory.' Mike took a deep breath.

'Come on, girl. I've got a car outside. The address is Castlepark, near Drogheda, County Louth.'

4

Malcolm McGill had had an undistinguished career in the Royal Air Force. Dreams of guiding his crippled bomber home through the dazzle of German searchlights had alternated with pictures of the dare-devil fighter leaping with gay abandon into Hurricane or Spitfire. The reality had been pay officer in a suburb of Newcastle-on-Tyne. By the end of the war he had, chiefly through the passing of time, attained the rank of Squadron-Leader. He had married a Colonel's daughter fumblingly seduced in an air-raid shelter. They had two children, a boy and a girl. After the war, with his father-in-law's influence, he managed to get a job as golf club secretary near Camberley. Margaret went back like a homing pigeon to coffee parties and bridge afternoons with Mummy. George and

Heather were dumped uncomplainingly at nursery school.

Malcolm had struggled along for five years, finding himself outranked in the Club and outplayed on the course, when he unexpectedly inherited an Irish mansion. Castlepark had belonged to his elder brother Johnny, who had bought the estate as a training establishment and died when a novice hunter cracked him into a stone wall at a point-to-point. His wife Jill was killed in a car crash on her way home from the funeral. Some said that she'd always taken that corner too fast. Her nearest friend held that she'd taken an appalled look at the years ahead and decided there was nothing for her without Johnny, not even their only child.

*   *   *

Mike drove his Aston-Martin across the Boyne as the clocks both sides of the river were striking midday. He manoeuvred expertly through Drogheda's narrow streets and finally drew up outside a modest hotel. Karen looked at him. 'Thirsty?'

'Look, Karen, it's better if I go on alone. My father's quite well known in these parts and I'm much more likely to get co-operation as an Adair than you as a stranger.' He leaned over and opened her door. 'This is the best pub for miles around. Everyone turns up sooner or later. Buy yourself a drink and insinuate Castlepark into the conversation. Choosing your moment, of course . . . '

'I did have some training,' said Karen frostily. It wasn't that she minded being edged out of the star rôle, it was the feeling that if anyone was going to discover anything to Greg's disadvantage, she should be the one. And yet — what approach could she possibly use other than straightforward question and answer? Mike was right. She got out of the car and smiled at him.

'I'll wait for you,' she said. 'And

— good luck.' She watched the car turn right and up the hill towards the north. Then she tied a scarf, peasant-fashion, over her hair, put on her sunglasses and opened the front door of Mooney's Hotel.

The bar was low-ceilinged, narrow and comfortably crowded. Two elderly women sat at a table at the far end, drinking Guinness. Otherwise the clientele was exclusively male. Playing inconspicuous, Karen ordered a beer and lit a cigarette, her face turned away from the light, her dark blue denim jeans and jacket merging into the corner near the door. After listening for five minutes to the voices around her, she worked out that the three men next to her were horse-copers from Cork and the next two commercial travellers staying at the hotel. From the other end of the bar she could hear disjointed phrases from an animated discussion of a local murder. A burst of cackling laughter told her that the two elderly harpies were joining in. Maybe that, after all, would be her best bet. Those two looked as if Mooney's had been home for a long, long time. She bought a Guinness, by-passed two golfers who had just come in and made her way to the table at the far end.

'Do you mind if I join you?' she asked diffidently.

Murder unsolved, conversation veered.

'You'd think,' mourned the grey-haired woman, black-shawled, 'that the Irish could recognize a con man when they see one.'

'How long ago was it? Three years? He must have been a foreigner or he'd have been recognized, wouldn't he? Wonder what he did with the money.' That was the one with the ferocious red wig. 'Always kind to old ladies, he was!' She cackled again.

Karen's involuntary movement almost knocked over her glass. That phrase and the time element . . . And the money to set up Carnlough Books?

'Are ye sure there's nothin' wrong?' Two pairs of gimlet eyes suddenly focussed on her face. 'Passin' through, are ye?'

'Yes. That is — I was looking for Castlepark,' said Karen, unnerved.

'Then you're in luck,' chimed in the landlord just behind her, 'because that's George McGill over there by the door.'

The subtle approach, Mike had advised. Choose your moment, he'd said. Karen swung round wildly. One of the golfers had also turned and was looking in her direction. He was a hefty man with black hair growing low on his forehead. Was she imagining a faint look of Greg about the eyes? There wasn't time to follow that line of thought because suddenly he was there in front of her. A quick glance took her in from headscarf to platform soles.

'If you're a reporter, at least you're an improvement on the last one,' he said unpleasantly.

5

Mike Adair wasn't nearly as sanguine as he'd led Karen to believe. Not least because he had very little idea what he was going to say to the owners of Castlepark. If Gavin McGill and Greg Marshall were one and the same, asking questions was going to be tricky.

★ ★ ★

Margaret McGill was having one of her bad days. This took the form, until she retired to her room with what she called My Migraine, of bitter resentment at her surroundings. Her husband retired thankfully to the stableyard, George escaped to the golf course at Baltray. As Heather had made an unfortunate marriage some years previously and was no longer invited to stay, the luckless recipient was, as ever, Bridie Muldoon.

Bridie had worked every weekday morning at Castlepark for over twenty-five years. She was getting ready to leave that Thursday noon when Margaret walked into the kitchen.

'The master said I could go a bit early,' she said defensively. Most of Bridie's sentences began with an excuse or an apology: a drunken father and six loutish brothers had seen to that.

'There's something you've forgotten,' said Margaret sharply. The silly woman was sure to fall into that little trap. Bridie did.

'It wasn't my fault. Would ye be meanin' the tea-pot that got broke?'

'No, I didn't mean the tea-pot,' Margaret said impatiently. She had already mislaid the point of the conversation. She surveyed the stone floor and scrubbed wooden table with distaste. She was sick to death of this large inconvenient house set in a howling wilderness as far as civilized amenities were concerned. She thought longingly of Mummy's blue and white

kitchen at Camberley with the match-
ing stools at the breakfast bar. Long
cosy bridge afternoons, tempting little
television suppers.

An old-fashioned bell jangled above
her head. Margaret turned abruptly and
strode out into the draughty corridor. If
this was another tradesman with the
nerve to use the front door . . .

★ ★ ★

As he drove up the short avenue, two
things immediately eased the situation
from Mike's point of view. The first was
that Castlepark was evidently a training
establishment. The second, now that he
could see the christian name of the
owner on the board inside the iron
gates, that he'd heard the man mentioned by his father. He parked the car
on the gravel sweep and walked up the
steps to the front door.

His first impression of Mrs McGill
was that he had never seen a meaner
mouth. The second — that she was

114

expecting someone else. He saw her expression change with dramatic rapidity as she took in the casual elegance of the Aston-Martin.

'I'm afraid George is out, but if you'd like to come in . . . ' George. So that was the name of the son and presumably about his own age. Mike followed her into a high-ceilinged hall and through to the drawing-room at the back of the house. Even a welter of busy chintz, he reflected, could not mar the generous proportions.

'As it happens, I came to see your husband, but maybe you can help me.' He paused. 'What a lovely house you have. Georgian, isn't it?'

Margaret's dislike of anything this side of the Irish Sea warred with appreciation of this tribute to her own good taste. Graciousness finally triumphed.

'Won't you sit down, Mr — Er . . . '

'Michael Adair. My father is Lord Tullamore and, I believe, known to your husband.' He looked at the regular features under the discreetly tinted hair and found he could read all too clearly what was going through her mind. There Macolm was, mucking about in the filthy stable-yard, oblivious of the inestimable social advantages of acquaintance with the aristocracy. Even in Ireland, a lord is a lord.

'Maybe Lady Tullamore . . . ?' hinted Margaret McGill.

Mike thought of his father, that most democratic of peers, interested only in schooling his hunters, living in the kitchen because it was the only warm room in the vast pile he called home.

'I'm afraid my mother is dead,' he said, striving to keep his voice even. He still missed her too. He rarely went back to Ballyteggart now.

As he opened his mouth to speak again, he had a sudden blinding vision of a future there with a new chatelaine, someone with gaiety and courage and ash-blonde hair. It disappeared as quickly as it had come but it left him with a conviction that it would return

116

again. And again.

'What I really wanted to ask your husband,' he improvised with scarcely a break, 'was about a man who has applied for the job as manager at Ballyteggart. But equally well, of course, you might know him. His name is Gavin McGill.' That was a hit. That really went home. Before she could stop herself, Margaret blurted out 'It can't be! He's in . . . ' Mike remained silent, face expressionless, waiting. In gaol? In Nether Wallop? Incurable? But Margaret had been brought up on military principles. Evacuating an impossible position was one of them. Initiating an outflanking movement was another.

'You must forgive me,' she intoned, 'for not offering you a drink. I'm afraid the staff . . . Perhaps a glass of sherry? No?' She looked at him with implacable eyes. 'I'm afraid that I can't help you. I did once know someone of that name but it couldn't possibly be the same man.'

Mike knew when he was beaten.

There was nothing more to be learnt from this source. He wondered, as he turned towards the door, if Malcolm was anywhere near the stables. There must be another drive that led round that way . . .

This time it was Margaret's turn for thought-reading.

'I'm afraid my husband will be in Dublin all day,' she said smoothly. She stood at the top of the steps till the car was out of sight. Then she walked quickly back through the house into the kitchen, out through the back door and along the lane which led to the stableyard.

6

'I didn't really take to George McGill,' said Karen. 'I don't care if I never have another Guinness either.' They were eating steak at a bar in Shop Street.

'You didn't tell me how you got away,' Mike reminded her.

'Well, I asked him what gave him the idea I looked like a reporter and while he was thinking up the answer to that, the opposition turned up — that is, the two missing members of the fourball — and George was swept off to play golf. I never did find out why they have reporters at Castlepark.'

'Probably another Arkle being trained there,' said Mike. 'There's always another Arkle being trained somewhere in Ireland ... Anyway, from all that Mrs McGill didn't say, I'm now satisfied that Gavin McGill is real, not just a statistic, a name on an airline manifest. Whether he turns out to be your husband . . . ' His tongue stumbled over the last two words.

'What do you want to do this afternoon?' he asked abruptly.

Karen picked up her handbag. Then she answered the question.

'I noticed the offices of the Drogheda Independent just down the street,' she said quickly. 'I thought I'd have a look at their back numbers.' She didn't tell him about Greg being kind to old ladies. She didn't mention the con man who had apparently got away with a lot of money just over three years ago. What was it, after all, but bar-room gossip? If no-one had been charged, it probably wouldn't even rate a couple of lines in the paper. But she couldn't afford to overlook any possible source of information.

'In that case,' said Mike, sensing she wanted to be alone, 'I might have a word with George when he's finished burning up the course at Baltray.'

★ ★ ★

George McGill was a bad loser. His temper wasn't improved by the sight of the gleaming Aston Martin outside the clubhouse. It intensified the humiliation of having to rely on his friends any time his father or mother needed the family car. It highlighted the ridiculous wage his father was paying him. No wonder he had to look for outside sources of revenue. Usually he could count on winning a tenner at golf, but today he hadn't played with his usual concentration. There was something about that female in the pub that worried him . . . Good figure too — he'd like to see her stripped. He gulped down a double whisky and ordered a round. At least his credit was good.

After the second drink, downed as quickly as the first, he looked about him for the owner of the Aston Martin. There were players he'd known over the last twenty years, men like himself who were able to slip an afternoon's golf into a working week, plus some outsiders from neighbouring courses and the odd tourist. None of the casuals looked as if they owned a useful handicap, let alone an expensive car. He turned back to the three other members of the fourball, thinking sourly it was about time one of the opposition ordered the next round. He'd need a lot more than a couple of whiskeys to get him through the boredom of another family evening at Castlepark. At that moment, someone behind brushed against his right elbow. He swung round, ready to snarl.

'So sorry.' It was a sandy-haired man in corduroys and a cotton sweater. 'Did I knock your glass? Do let me get you another.'

George McGill, Mike decided ten minutes later, was a pushover. After another whiskey, there was little Mike didn't know about habits of father, mother, sister, stableboys, horses and someone called Bridie Muldoon. Mike ordered what he reckoned was the fifth

John Jameson and put his question before befuddled loquacity should become befuddled suspicion.

'Gavin isn't a relation then?' he put in casually. George didn't react as his mother had. George didn't react at all.

'Gavin? Don't know anyone by that name. Wait . . . wait a minute . . . ' He swayed forward on the balls of his feet. 'Had a cousin or something, long time ago. Dis — disappeared . . . '

That was all he was going to get. Mike dumped the intoxicated George in the vicinity of his hardly less convivial golfing chums and drove fast along the north bank of the Boyne back to Drogheda. The tide was running strongly upriver, bearing a Norwegian cargo vessel. A Belfast-bound train rumbled over the viaduct. He parked the car in the centre of the town and strolled down Shop Street. Gavin, he reckoned, must be the son of Malcolm McGill's brother, the one who had died in a hunting accident. He wondered what had happened to the mother. Had she died too? Then surely Castlepark would have been left in trust for Gavin? Had Gavin McGill alias Greg Marshall, come back to claim his inheritance?

⋆   ⋆   ⋆

Karen didn't expect to find anything in the back numbers of the Drogheda Independent. So she wasn't disappointed when nothing relevant to the case turned up in any issue dated April or May, nineteen seventy-three. She was on the point of closing the file when the word Castlepark caught her eye. The item was merely a few lines tucked away at the bottom of an inside page. It stated that Paddy Muldoon had been arrested at Tullybeg for being drunk and disorderly while in charge of a bicycle, the said vehicle being the property of his daughter, Bridie, who had worked at Castlepark since she was a girl of fifteen.

It didn't say how old she was now,

but the assumption was that she had worked there for more years than she cared to remember. If anyone knew the skeletons in the McGill family cupboard, surely it must be Bridie Muldoon.

7

Paddy Mudoon was drunk again. The money he had removed from his daughter's purse was oiling the way to oblivion in O'Neill's bar up the road and Bridie was alone in the cottage.

Mike parked the car in a gateway down the lane. He and Karen stood looking at the downtrodden patch of weed that was the front garden. The door was closed, but a wisp of smoke trailed from the chimney.

'Maybe she'll give us a cup of tea,' suggested Karen. She didn't move.

'Maybe she'll give us the answer,' said Mike.

He had been prepared for lack of comprehension, refusal, even abuse. What he hadn't expected was recognition.

'Mister Michael! Ye've grown just like your father. Ye don't remember the time he brought ye to Castlepark? Well, ye couldn't have been more than three at the time. And is this your wife? Come in, now.'

They followed her into the kitchen with the peat fire and the griddle and the tea-pot on the hob.

'Was Gavin there at the time?' Mike asked casually.

'No. That was after . . . ' Her hand went to her mouth in ludicrous parody of Margaret McGill.

'You might as well tell us, Bridie,' said Mike gently. 'It won't go any further than the two of us — and a lot more harm might be done asking questions round the countryside.'

Bridie Muldoon sat down at the table and twisted the hem of her apron in her red work-gnarled hands. A moment ago she had been hostess to two visitors in her own kitchen with her father out of the way and her brothers with wives of their own to knock about. Now she was the maid-of-all-work at Castlepark, faced by the sin of omission that had haunted her over the last twenty-five years.

'It was the Will,' she whispered.

Gavin, son of Johnny and Jill, had been orphaned when he was two years old. By the terms of the Will deposited some five years previously at Johnny's bank in Drogheda, Castlepark and the money to maintain the estate went to his brother Malcolm. When a later Will, leaving everything to Gavin, was discovered in the house, Malcolm and Margaret — after some deliberation — consigned it to the drawing-room fire. It was the deliberation that was overheard by Bridie Muldoon, polishing floor boards in the room next door.

'I should have gone to the Garda,' said Bridie, 'but I was scared of losin' the job. Me Da would have killed me.' So Margaret struck a bargain. Bridie could continue to work at Castlepark for as long as she liked, providing she kept her mouth shut. A bargain indeed, thought Mike with sudden anger, that was entirely in Margaret McGill's favour. She had solved the servant problem with one sentence and transferred the burden of conscience as well.

'What happened to Gavin?' asked Karen. The words were the first she had spoken.

'It was said he went to his mother's people. But I know better. They sent him away for adoption. Far away.' As far away as Canada?

Bridie couldn't remember where, it was all so long ago.

'But he turned up again. How inconvenient,' murmured Mike.

'Aye, about three years ago. I heard tell he had a wife or was getting married, but I think he left her in England.' The girl from Leeson Park? Or the one who was waiting in Barnscombe?

Now the worst of the confession was over, Bridie rallied sufficiently to fill three tea-cups from the pot on the hob. Karen thankfully gulped the bitter brew.

'Do you know why he came back?' she asked.

'Maybe to see the place where he was

born. Maybe hopin' for money. I could have told him there wouldn't be any of that comin' in his direction. He only came to Castlepark the once and he only saw the missus.'

'Did you see him, Bridie?'

'I did. T'was meself that opened the door to him.'

'Do you remember what he looked like?' Karen found she was holding her breath as she waited for the answer.

'Sure I remember, seein' it was the last time I saw him before he drowned himself.'

★　★　★

The car ate up the miles between Tullybeg and Dublin.

'So he just walked out into the sea,' said Mike, 'leaving a neat little pile of clothes on the beach. I wonder why. I'll bet that Margaret has a good idea. The one thing I'll never know,' he ended regretfully, 'is how she would have finished that sentence.'

130

8

'We've only lived with them for a day and George is the only one I've talked to — if you could call it a conversation.' Karen stared dreamily out of the window. 'And yet I feel I know them better than my own family.'

'They would have been your own family,' pointed out Mike, 'if you'd been right in the first place. You might find nastier in-laws but I doubt it.'

Dusk was shadowing the corners of O'Connell Street when they drew up outside the hotel.

'I've only known you for twenty-eight hours,' said Mike. 'It isn't enough for me, Karen.' She turned her head and looked at him. His eyes were hazel and his mouth was wide and generous. She found she couldn't look away. His arms closed round her shoulders and her mouth met his with a shock of recognition. 'Mike. Oh Mike.'

His flat was on the top floor of an old house near Merrion Square. That grey, misty June weekend, it seemed as divorced from reality as her imaginary picture of the castle where he'd been born. She only knew that they created a world of their own, without thought of the past or concern for the future.

'I don't even know what you do,' she told him, frying bacon on Saturday morning. Surely bacon had never been so appetizing before.

'A television writer in search of a plot,' he answered, pouring coffee into earthenware mugs. 'I think, you know, that you've just given me one. I might follow it up.' He drew up two wooden chairs. 'I never knew bacon could smell like this, did you?' Outside a soft rain was falling.

'We'll go to the races,' said Mike.

On Sunday they drove into the Wicklow Mountains.

'Life is not complete,' said Mike, 'till you've stood in the Vale of Avoca.'

On Monday morning he woke her from a sleep of deep contentment and told her he had to go away. 'Plane for Casablanca this afternoon. They just phoned me. A kind director needs a scriptwriter for a film about Bogart. I'll fly with you to London.'

They drank champagne over the Irish Sea and talked spasmodically. Weeks afterwards Karen remembered disjointed words, even whole sentences. At London Airport he held her tight and wished from the bottom of his tormented heart that he hadn't had the strength of will to send her away.

'You're not going to Casablanca, are you? You're going back to Ireland. You made it all up,' Karen said shakily, her head on his shoulder, eyes closed to hide the tears.

'Yes, my love. It's a lie. Kind directors are like leprechauns — never yet encountered.' He handed her his handkerchief. 'Two days? A week? A month? It's no good. I need a lifetime.'

Karen opened her eyes. They were

standing not twenty yards from the place Greg had left her that April day over three years ago. In a moment Mike too would walk away, waving goodbye, turning towards the Aer Lingus check-in.

Only, of course, Greg hadn't gone to Ireland after all. A man called Gavin McGill had travelled to Dublin that day, never to return. The whole thing had been a gigantic charade, a game of bending the facts to fit the theory. In practical terms, the exercise had got her precisely nowhere. She raised her head and looked at Mike.

'Where do I go from here?'

*   *   *

Back in Oakley Street, Karen sat drinking black coffee because she'd forgotten to buy any milk. Buying milk belonged to normal everyday life. The feeling of being exposed to a cold wind had been with her ever since Mike had turned away. That comes of being totally committed to one person and I wouldn't recommend it to anyone, she told herself fiercely. Unless they've a reasonable expectation of spending the rest of their lives together.

That afternoon, she got down to planning her next move. First of all she phoned Torquay and got the same answer as last time. There had been no communication from Greg, or from anyone connected with Barnscombe. She had a sudden vision of them all — Greg, Jenny, Mark, Tim — carrying on with the daily business of living as if she, Karen, had never existed. Or as if she were dead. That last picture made her face reality as nothing else could have done. Someone had wished her dead. Someone, presumably, still did.

'Every plot has its logic,' Mike had reminded her at the airport. 'Haven't you rather lost sight of first principles? What you want to discover is whether he had a motive.' And you aren't likely to find it, had been the implication, in Canada or Ireland, but much nearer home. Just before he left, he'd asked her a question.

'Have you made a Will, Karen? No? Well, have you looked at the small print in your mother's?'

That, in the end, turned out to be the only clue that mattered.

JENNY

1

Karen sat in a London bus and forced herself to think about Jenny. The problem as always was to decide where to begin, other than the mists of childhood. Her aunt and uncle in Sevenoaks would only know the face Jenny presented to them. Even the girls she had lived with would have been unlikely to probe beneath the surface. Doubtless they had their own problems. The only hope was that a clue might emerge from casual conversation. So she went to Holland Park.

She couldn't remember the names of the two girls with whom Jenny had once shared a flat but she did know the address. Six o'clock in the evening seemed a reasonable time to call — not too soon for at least one of them to be home from work, time enough to catch them if they were going out later. That is, assuming they were still there . . .

She recognized the names as soon as she saw the card slotted under the second floor bell. T. Evans and F. McMurdo. Tracy and Fiona. When she reached the door of the flat, she saw a tall girl with brown, curly hair. There was something about her that fitted the name.

'Fiona McMurdo? I'm Jenny's sister. May I come in?'

Fiona was twenty-five and a model. She had an oval face and a faint Scottish accent. She was engagingly friendly.

'Is Jenny still down in Exeter or wherever? We didn't let her room, as you see. It's all gracious living now we have a guest room. In the old days you kept falling over bodies sleeping on the sitting-room floor. Jenny's Tim once kipped in the bath. Would you like a drink?'

Karen accepted Dubonnet with lemon and ice. She took a tentative sip.

'Tim?' she said slowly. 'I didn't know . . . '

'Tim Malone. The actor. Tracy and I went to see his new play the other night. Rather dishy, isn't he? He used to come here quite a lot.'

Tracy came in after a few minutes — small, blonde, bouncy.

'You don't look a bit like Jenny, do you? Actually, we only just knew that she had a sister. She never talked about her family. How about her book? We've been expecting to see it festooned round the local W. H. Smith, haven't we, Fi? She did mention someone called Mark who might be interested in publishing it. And just before she left, she went to look up his wife — ex-wife? — name of Judy anyway, at some earnest university like Reading or Durham. How about another drink?'

* * *

Karen sat on the top deck of a bus bound for the West End and considered her findings. That Jenny had contacted

Mark's divorced wife was only confirmation of a suspicion that her sister had planned her visit to Barnscombe with some care. That she had been on such friendly terms with Tim Malone was both annoying and disturbing. True, she knew that Jenny had originally met him at a party in Hampstead. But subsequently she had been led to believe that they only encountered each other — and that entirely by chance — at The Salthouse. It was annoying because they had deceived her. It was disturbing because she could see no reason why they should have kept their relationship a secret.

She got off the bus in Piccadilly and walked through Green Park in the direction of Knightsbridge, Sloane Square, King's Road, Oakley Street. It was a long walk but it would help to fill in the empty hours till bedtime. There was nothing more she could find out about Jenny tonight. She was more than halfway across Green Park before she suspected she was being followed.

Glancing round quickly, she realized there was no tangible reason for such a suspicion. The only symptom was a tingling sensation at the nape of her neck. The sun had gone down into a long bank of cloud, the air was warm and still. It was now too late for the homegoing throng of businessmen, civil servants and typists and too early for the theatre crowds. But strollers and lovers were everywhere — on the paths, under the trees, lying on the grass. Anyone could be watching her. She shrugged her shoulders and walked on.

People in Knightsbridge were thinner on the ground. Sloane Street was practically deserted. Acting on impulse, she darted through the imposing entrance of a block of flats and forced herself to walk purposefully up the central staircase. She stood at the head of the first flight and listened. Nobody followed her in. The only sound was intermittent traffic. But if anyone had followed and attacked her, would anyone hear her scream? Or were the dwellers insulated by thick pile carpets, double glazing, soundproof walls against any but their own little world? She slipped down the stairs again and out into the comparative safety of the street. A man walked by on the other side. Two girls in long skirts crossed the road, laughing. There was a group of people down near Sloane Square. She walked on.

The feeling persisted. Turning her head quickly while on a traffic island in the middle of King's Road, she thought she recognized the outline of a man's head and shoulders but the impression, so fleeting, had disappeared by the time she reached the pavement. Once in Oakley Street, she ran. No pounding footsteps echoed her own.

She locked the door of her apartment and stood, shielded by the curtain, looking out of the window. It was some minutes before she moved back into the room and poured a generous tot from a bottle of John Jameson which Mike had given her.

★ ★ ★

The man in the saloon bar of the
Phoenix opposite number 117 finished
his drink. He ordered another one and
waited for the shadows outside to
deepen into dusk.

2

It was Margo Peters who provided an unexpected lead. Karen had deliberated for some time before calling on the fashion editor of 'Denim', chiefly because Margo had a cottage at Torbay and not infrequently visited Barnscombe. On the other hand, the odds against her running into Greg were considerable. There was no reason why she should know how things stood at the moment.

Margo's first words dispelled any doubts.

'Hullo, Karen! All well in Barnscombe? I haven't been down to the cottage for months — since the Anstruther sherry party, in fact. I'm getting married next month and going to live in America.' Margo's perfectly made-up eyes rarely gave anything away but for a brief moment Karen was aware of a deep satisfaction. She also realized how fortunately she had timed her visit. Margo was so absorbed by her own happiness that she showed no surprise at the appearance of Jenny's sister more than a year after Jenny had left 'Denim'. She answered without extraneous comment the carefully phrased questions about contacts and friends but pointed out that Jenny had been in a different department and they'd really had little in common. 'Funny thing, though!' she went on, 'I was clearing out the junk in my desk the other day and I came across a note she wrote me last December. It was a scrawl asking if there were any openings in my department. Well, there weren't — and what with Christmas and all, I forgot to answer it. But I do remember the address. It was Calthorpe House, Exeter.'

Last December. That was roughly two or three months after she, Karen, had warned her sister to stay away from Barnscombe. She hadn't caught up with Jenny again till early spring. Even then, Jenny had volunteered no information as to what she'd been doing the preceding six months. There was only the rumour of 'a fabulous job in the west country.' At Calthorpe House?

*   *   *

Another journey, a new objective. Karen reached Exeter at mid-afternoon on the last day of June. On the principle of expecting the best service at the best places, she took a taxi to the Royal Western in Cathedral Close and booked a room for the night. Then she tackled the head porter.

'Calthorpe House, madam? Can't say I know it. Could be a new block of flats, of course. Going up all the time. I'll check for you in the directory, madam.'

Calthorpe House was not a block of flats. It wasn't a hotel, either, or a boarding house. If it was a private address, the name of the owner wasn't Calthorpe.

'It could, I suppose,' said the porter

doubtfully, 'be business premises hous-
ing several concerns but not to my
knowledge.' He fingered the ends of his
grey moustache. Mr Brewer didn't like
to be outpointed. He had lived all his
life, apart from the war years, in or
around Exeter, and no one had yet caught
him out on topography. 'Tell you what,'
he said suddenly, 'there's a small village
called Calthorpe just outside the city on
the Dunsford road. Maybe there's been
some building done there recently or
maybe the big house has now been bought.
It used to be The Cedars, as I remember. You didn't come by car, madam?
Well, there's a bus from the station,
every half hour, I think it is . . . '

★   ★   ★

It was high noon and the hamlet of
Calthorpe was deserted. The green bus
disappeared round the corner and
silence descended on half a dozen
terraced houses and a small honey-
coloured pub. The sun beat down from

a cloudless sky. Karen dived thankfully for the gloom of the Horseshoe and ordered a long gin and tonic. Half-an-hour later she was standing on the doorstep of Calthorpe House Clinic.

The receptionist was an olive-skinned girl with dark hair swept into a coil on top of her head. She wore a starched white coat, and a white band round her smooth head. She looked cool and efficient. Karen was hot and tired and afraid of what she was going to find out. Because something had happened to Jenny here, she was certain of that. Something which had changed her in an indefinable way.

'Good morning,' she said lightly. 'I really did mean to call sooner than this but I've been abroad for some time. The thing is, my sister thought she'd left a book of mine here and this is the first time I've been near Exeter for months . . . ' How easy it was to rattle on, she thought, getting nowhere, putting off the moment of discovery. The girl raised an eyebrow.

'Your sister was a patient?' She had a faint accent. French? Probably.

'She was here towards the end of last year. Jenny Hobson.'

'Ah — Jenny!' The girl smiled. 'She took over from me for a month when my mother in Lyons had an accident. We were lucky she was free at the time.'

So that was it. Jenny had wanted a temporary job and happened to be on the spot when the girl had to return to France. And when she . . . 'My name is Monique' . . . was due to come back to her job, Jenny had written to Margot to see if she could find another opening in 'Denim'. It was all very simple. Except for one thing. Why had Jenny come to Exeter in the first place?

'That was after the abortion, of course,' said Monique placidly.

Karen had no time to hide her face. The shock was instantly apparent.

'You didn't know! I am so sorry. But I was sure that it was her brother-in-law who brought her here.'

151

3

Greg's baby. There could be no other explanation. The seduction scene had been September, the abortion November. The only important question now, thought Karen numbly, was who had made the decision — Greg or Jenny?

Looking back, she realized that she and Greg had rarely talked about children. Before they got married, they had agreed not to start a family for at least a year. That period had been tacitly extended while Greg was building up the firm: the house might be hers but he insisted on being responsible for all other expenditure. Then Jenny had come to stay and a subtle air of tension had invaded even the large double bedroom. Yet instinctively she knew that Greg wanted a son. Why, then, had he not asked for a divorce so that he could marry Jenny?

A monstrous suspicion for the first time forced itself to the forefront of her mind. Had he been playing for higher stakes? Had he schemed to have both Jenny and the Hobson inheritance?

*   *   *

Karen found she was sitting on a hardbacked chair holding a glass of water. Monique was talking on the telephone. A nurse walking through the hall gave her an incurious glance. Presumably white-faced women with glasses of water were part of her daily life. Karen drank the water thirstily and got to her feet. Monique put down the receiver and made a note on the pad in front of her.

'Can I do anything to help you?' she asked.

'Not really,' said Karen. What use was practised sympathy against the fact of betrayal? 'But thank you.' She could hear a car coming up the drive.

Monique was turning away.

'Oh, just one thing. I think she was expecting a letter. Did she leave a forwarding address?' Monique, obviously relieved to be spared histrionics, flipped expertly through a ledger.

'The Salthouse, Barnscombe,' she read out.

Karen sat down on a grassy bank opposite the Horseshoe and waited for the next bus back to Exeter. The sun blazed down and her head felt empty. There was something, though, that had to be worked out. Jenny had left Calthorpe House a week before Christmas, giving Barnscombe as the address for letters to be forwarded. And she had been expecting a letter, an important one from her point of view as she had been hoping to get another job with 'Denim'. Yet surely, if she'd been in touch with Greg, she must have known about the holiday in Austria? Karen counted back from December twenty-fifth the previous year — yes, they must have left England on Tuesday the twenty-first. And that could only mean that Jenny, still hoping to hear from Margo Peters, had lived — or at least called in most days — at The Salthouse while they had been away. Had Greg had a key especially cut for her or had he given her his own?

What a ridiculous situation, Karen thought suddenly, her own sister sneaking into the family home because she was too proud to ask if she could stay there while she and Greg were in Austria. That Jenny might have scruples about using the house occurred briefly to Karen and was instantly dismissed. Jenny didn't have that sort of scruple.

The bus was nearly empty. Karen got off at the station to enquire about trains back to London. She was passing a small bookshop next to the building when a familiar trademark caught her eye — two capital letters encircling a lighted candle. Carnlough Books. Honiton, of course, was not far away: presumably Exeter was their main distribution centre. This display included text books, a couple of biographies, a volume of wartime anecdotes, three historical romances and a modern novel. The novel was entitled 'Only One Can Play'. The author was Jenny Hobson.

The afternoon train for London slid out of the station and disappeared into the heat haze. Karen wasn't there to see it go. The comfortable voice of a Devon-born announcer advised that the next one would leave from platform five at six-twenty. Karen wasn't listening. She was in the bookshop, handing over three pound notes and getting back ten pence in change.

She walked back to the Royal Western and ordered a pot of coffee in her room. Then she sat down on the bed and opened the book.

4

The main character in 'Only One Can Play' was a young man who knew exactly where he was going and didn't mind how he got there. Brought up in a Nottingham slum, his only talent a natural eye for a ball, he graduated from wasteground bashing to junior Nottingham Rangers. From then on, for Jimbo, it was the big league.

Jenny's acquaintance with Nottingham was probably limited to a one-day trip, her knowledge of football conned from a couple of Saturdays on the terraces. But where fact left off, imagination took over, all of it believable, all of it written in the idiom of the day. The main theme was singleness of purpose, From the moment Jimbo was sent off for offering friendly advice to the referee, one knew that one day he was going to join the England squad.

157

Stealing from his Mum, cheating his sister, ditching his girl, mutilating a rival — all the way he jinked with retribution and won. Lank-haired and lantern-jawed, undervalued from birth, he used his seeming inadequacies as a weapon as potent as his magical left boot. His final cry for help was the seduction of his brother's wife in the back of his Mercedes.

Karen read the hundred and ninety-seven pages in less than two hours. There was no doubt that Jenny could write. The narrative had verve and impetus, the style was crisp. She also had an ear for dialogue of the monosyllabic variety. All this Karen adjudged without actually putting it into words. What really held her enthralled from the birth of the unwanted Jimbo, through his under-privileged childhood, to the scene of his greatest triumph was a growing conviction that the novel was autobiographical.

Karen thought about her sister. Jenny could never have described herself as unwanted, but she couldn't have helped knowing that her father had set his heart on a son. There were few material advantages she lacked in childhood — yet she might have missed the continuity denied to Service children. Though she had had no occasion to steal or mutilate as she clawed her way onto the first rung of the ladder, the potential was there. She had tried to cheat her sister, she had seduced her brother-in-law. She had the same physical characteristics as her anti-hero. She would almost certainly do anything to attain her ambition.

Karen reviewed her assessment with something like horror. Was Jenny really like that? If she was, there was no evading the hypothesis that in her world an obstacle was there to be removed. In other words, it could have been Jenny — either acting alone or in collusion — who had instigated three near-accidents within the space of nine months. If it was a solo effort, there must be a reservation concerning the Austrian incident. Or . . . must there? There was no proof that Jenny was in Barnscombe over Christmas or indeed in England. If she had a collaborator — who could it be but Greg?

★ ★ ★

Before she went to bed, Karen forced herself to read the book through again from beginning to end. When she awoke to the sound of birdsong in Cathedral Close and looked across the roofs to another perfect dawn, she found that optimism had returned. Somewhere in the reaches of the night, her brain had come up with an entirely new angle. Over a blessedly early cup of tea, she thought about it.

The premise was that Jenny's character, apart from certain not unusual aspects such as reserve, egotism and perhaps a touch of malice, was that of a normal twenty-three-year-old somewhat deficient in family feeling. This last was only to be expected in someone

160

who had been a second and less favoured daughter. She was a born writer with a natural desire to be recognized. Right? All very reasonable so far.

The next step was the novel. Jenny had started writing 'Only One Can Play' when she was eighteen or nineteen. In those days, Greg hadn't even entered their lives. So the sister-in-law ploy was probably just imagination. It was true that Jenny — after the book's return from various publishing houses — had revised several times. But the point was that no episode had necessarily been based on Greg as a person. There might be shades of autobiography in the book, but then they say that's true of most first novels, don't they?

Karen finished her tea and lit a cigarette. The activities of the present day Jenny took rather more explaining away. Her method of getting financial backing could hardly be dignified by the epithet fraudulent but in essence that's what it was. Then there was the affair with Greg and the subsequent abortion. As evidence of character not commendable, but not rare in this permissive age. What was Jenny, in fact, but an innocuous entry in a social worker's casebook?

* * *

This mood of near-benevolence stayed with Karen all the way back to London. It lasted till she opened the envelope waiting for her on the hall table at 117 Oakley Street. It was a long official envelope from Somerset House forwarding as requested a copy of her mother's Will.

Karen remembered her mother as a quiet and gentle person, the perfect complement to her forceful and ebullient father. Yet it was Mary Hobson who had been the centre of family life and Karen had missed her painfully. The Will had been drawn up several years before she died and was indicative of her loving concern for the future of her daughters. Karen reflected ironically that the reason she herself hadn't made a Will in the first three years of marriage was that death had seemed so far away: now that it had passed so close, whom could she trust with her inheritance?

She read slowly through the document in her hand. There was one provision she had entirely forgotten — if indeed she had ever taken it in. As soon as she had read it, she knew that she would never forget it again. In case of disablement, said the printed word, control of all monies would temporarily pass to Jenny Hobson with an established family friend as co-executor.

That was it. In a flash of enlightenment, Karen saw the answer to something which had puzzled her over the months — why a more certain method of disposal had not been used. A stormy sea, treacherous snow, cold stone — each was as likely to cause injury as death. Her next feeling was wry amusement that her mother's safeguard should have paved the way for a predator. The only positive outcome was the exclusion of Greg as partner-in-crime. For this rôle there were now but two qualifiers. Mark and Tim.

As for Jenny, she had been urgently in need of money. Karen looked down at the Will. What had been missing before was there in front of her. The motive.

TIM

1

There could only be one starting point in an appraisal of the life and character of Tim Malone and that was the theatre. Karen phoned an agency and was lucky to get a seat for 'Flashback' at the Serendipity the following night. She didn't mind going to a performance on her own. In fact, on this occasion she preferred to have no distraction. What she wanted to see was Tim through the eyes of an audience.

'Flashback' was the familiar story of an ageing actress facing the challenge of a rising star. It's popularity was due partly to the glamour of its leading lady, Philomena Johns, who fought a continually winning battle against the ravages of the years, and partly because of the author's cleverly contrived series of flashbacks. Tim played her leading man in the earlier episodes, her husband — increasingly attracted to the young Jan Patric — in the later. The critics had been divided in their reviews, but box-office takings assured a long run.

Karen, trained in punctuality, was in her seat five minutes before the curtain went up. As the row filled up, the seat beside her remained unoccupied. It wasn't till halfway through the first act that she realized someone had slipped in and was sitting on her left. She didn't need a second glance to recognize the well-known theatrical agent who had put Tim on the West End map. He too seemed to be gauging audience reaction. She turned her attention back to the stage.

★　★　★

The earlier flashbacks dealt with shows of the thirties, with Philomena apparently effortlessly portraying a girl of twenty-three and Tim a brash young man. The last two minutes of Act I showed them twenty years on, married and edgily competing for adulation. Jan Patric, as understudy, stood in the wings and awaited her chance.

★   ★   ★

In the first interval, her neighbour nipped off briskly in the direction of the bar. Karen went out to the foyer and lit a cigarette. She had seen enough to determine that the audience liked Tim Malone. He slid smoothly into his part. He didn't dominate but he had an easy professionalism. Probably most of them associated him with the successful Simon Harvard of 'Repertory' and he didn't let them down.

At the end of Act II, there was an unforgetable moment. The stage was in shadow, the spotlight on Tim standing near the wings. Another spot picked out Jan, drifting downstage. She was wearing jeans and a T-shirt. Her short dark hair lay like feathers on her forehead. Still vulnerable, still impressionable

— above all, young. Tim didn't speak. But the involuntary movement of his hands had a poignancy that words could never have achieved. There was an instant's total silence and then a storm or applause.

★ ★ ★

The theatrical agent clapped with more than routine enthusiasm. 'That always gets them!' he said with satisfaction. Karen turned her head, lips parted, eyes wide.

'You'd be a natural for Jan's part. You an actress? Come and have a drink.' He cleaved his way with authority through the crowd round the bar.

'How did you see that last scene?' he asked, handing her a glass.

'I thought,' said Karen slowly, 'that it was the only chance Miss Johns really allowed him.' Trevor Allen looked at her approvingly.

'You're right,' he said. 'He only got the part because Philomena wanted a leading man who couldn't steal the limelight, to coin a phrase.'

He had an aquiline nose, thinning dark hair and cultivated sideboards.

'Mind you, he's got a ruthless streak, has our boy. Otherwise she'd have cut the scene as soon as she realized how the audience was going to react. Another gin, sugar? There's lots of time. The curtain waits for theatrical agents.'

* * *

The play ended with Jan, now at the top, exhibiting the same single-minded concern for her career as the ageing Philomena, with Tim tiredly chatting up the latest newcomer. When the lights went up, Trevor Allen was greeted by a party of friends. Karen slipped quietly out into Shaftesbury Avenue.

2

For a moment she hesitated. It would only be a matter of minutes to find the stage door and be taken to Tim's dressing-room. She didn't doubt that he would be glad to see her. Or — would he? The evening was warm but suddenly she shivered. If he and Jenny really were collaborators, he would be glad to know she was in London. He might insist on accompanying her back to Oakley Street. He might even know already where she was living. She thought of the man who had followed her. But no, that couldn't possibly have been Tim, he would never have risked being late for curtain-up. Still, it hadn't been very clever of her to come to the theatre tonight. At any moment he might appear . . .

She eventually found a taxi outside the Piccadilly Hotel. As it wound its way towards Sloan Square, she totted up what she had learnt in the last couple of days. Tim knew Jenny better than he'd ever indicated. Tim had a ruthless streak. And that to the fact that Tim, until he'd landed the male lead in 'Flashback', had been badly in need of money, and it was reasonable to suppose that they had set up the plan together. But supposition was not enough. She had to have proof. And only by direct question could she find out if Jenny knew about the codicil in her mother's Will.

Karen unlocked the front door of 117 Oakley Street and closed it carefully behind her. Usually she went straight upstairs, but tonight for some reason she glanced at the letters on the hall table. She had met two or three of the other tenants on the stairs or the doorstep and she decided it might be interesting to fit the names to the faces. There was even at the back of her mind the unpleasant idea that someone living here might be keeping an eye on her

. . . There were half a dozen letters, a postcard and a magazine on the table. Karen stood still, hand half outstretched. Whatever she had been expecting, it wasn't this. Not an envelope addressed to her. Mrs Karen Marshall, 117 Oakley Street, London, S.W.3. The postmark was also S.W.3. The date was yesterday's. She didn't recognize the handwriting.

No-one, not even the twins, knew where she was living. She hadn't given her address . . . Oh but she had. She remembered the other letter she'd received, the one from Somerset House. Could somebody have got at her that way?

At least it wasn't a bomb. It wasn't thick enough for that. Karen picked it up and tore open the flap. There was a single piece of paper, written on both sides. The signature was 'Mike'.

The message was brief but oh so heartening. 'I didn't go back to Ireland — not immediately. There were three reasons. One — you gave me no address, just a reference to Albert

174

Bridge. I reckoned it had to be Oakley Street: so I waited there and followed you to Holland Park and back. Two — I had to reassure myself no-one else was following you. Three — if I frightened you, I meant to. The next time someone tails you, it won't be me. I said there were three reasons. There were four. You know the fourth. Goodbye, alannah.'

3

The Oetztal Alps stood out strong and clear against the summer sky. In Dornberg the sun was shining but the heat was tempered by the wind blowing down from the mountain tops. Wild poppies peppered the meadows. The water of the outdoor swimming pool was icy blue.

★   ★   ★

The morning after Mike's letter arrived, Karen had decided there was only one course open to her. As far as theory was concerned, she could go no further. The one practical thing she could do was to find out if Tim had been in Austria at the beginning of January. And the only person who could tell her that was Marisa Weingartner.

The airlines were fully booked this first weekend in July so she boarded the first available cross-Channel ferry and managed to get a seat on the Tauern Express. Changing at Schwarzach St. Veit in Tirol, she caught a local train and then a bus which meandered through the mountain villages. It was late afternoon when she reached Dornberg. Bypassing the hotel where she and Greg had stayed, Karen walked on beyond the onion-domed church and the last of the holiday villas to the Pension Arlberg. There was one room vacant on the second floor, a smiling girl in a dirndl informed her: it was at the back of the house, looking up at the peaks. Karen said it was exactly what she wanted. When she stood on the balcony, looking across the blaze of petunias to the path she had so painstakingly negotiated in the snow, she knew she had been right. Not a hundred metres above the Arlberg was the small white chalet where Marisa lived.

Breakfast was still coffee, hot rolls and black cherry jam. Karen ate it on the terrace overlooking the valley far below and tried to work out what she was going to say when she came face to face with Marisa. A reason for her presence here was easy enough to fabricate. Greg was on a business trip to Innsbruck and she had come up for a couple of days in the mountains. What more natural that she should look up someone who had stayed with them, especially as they'd so narrowly missed her last Christmas. As she sat there, she had a sudden vision of Tim as he'd looked, standing on the doorstep of The Salthouse, not long after their return from Dornberg. She remembered remarking on his tanned face and he'd said he'd acquired it playing golf with his producer. It hadn't struck her as odd at the time . . .

It was still early when she finished breakfast, too early for a casual call. So she wandered back into the village and took the cable car up to the top station.

It was cold up there, with cloud covering the peaks. Karen pulled on a sweater and started scrambling down the Blue Run.

At the bottom of the first drop, she turned and looked back. Odd how much steeper the gradient looked without its covering of snow. She practised an imaginary christie round the next corner and came to the top of the hill she had taken straight that January day. At that moment two fleeting impressions in her mind fused to form a single picture. The first was that dark blue shape she had noticed vanishing round the bend just before the accident: the second, the glimpse of Tim wearing dark blue jeans and sweater, silhouetted against the evening sky shortly after the return from Austria.

★ ★ ★

Suppose it were Tim who had changed over the arrows. That, as the Americans

179

say, figured. It was Tim's initiative. Marisa was merely, unknowingly or not, an accessory. She must have switched them back again and then disappeared into the woods en route for the chalet. Unknowingly? Hardly. But either she had blindly followed Tim's lead or else he had fed her the idea of the — harmless, of course — English practical joke. Karen couldn't believe there was any malice in Marisa.

Suddenly it seemed vital to find her as soon as possible.

4

The path was steep and bumpy. Karen could imagine Marisa gliding through the trees, banking at the corners, fast yet always perfectly controlled. Had she been controlled that day, at ease? Or had she been afraid that Tim was up to something she couldn't understand?

As she avoided rocky outcrops and slid around corners, Karen reflected on the split-second timing which had so nearly added up to an unpleasant accident. Tim and Marisa must have been concealed either in a hut or among the crowd of tourists at the top of the mountain. How easy, after all, to hide behind the hood of an anorak and a pair of goggles. When Greg had taken off, presumably they thought that he meant to do the run on his own. Tim then waited to see her, Karen, begin the descent, knowing he had plenty of time to bypass her, change the arrows and continue on down. Marisa had only to sweep down the Red Run to the junction and change them back. What turned it all into the sort of bedroom farce that had people popping in and out of cupboards with expert precision, thought Karen, was that Greg all this time had been waiting about fifty meters further down, just out of sight of the junction. If he'd come looking for her sooner . . . But, of course, he had expected her to be even slower than she was. It was her desire to impress him that had made the whole operation run so smoothly.

The path levelled as the trees thinned out and Karen emerged into warm sunlight. Just below she could see the red tiled roof of the Pension Arlberg. Right in front of her, on a small plateau hollowed out of the mountain-side, was Marisa's chalet.

As soon as she saw it, Karen knew that something was wrong. It wasn't only that the shutters were closed on a fine day in high summer. It wasn't the lack of window boxes, the subtle air of neglect. Just inside the front gate was a board on a post. You didn't have to be a linguist to know that 'Zu verkaufen' meant 'For Sale'.

The girl at the Pension Arlberg said she was sorry but she was only there for the summer months and she didn't know anything about a Fräulein Weingartner. The chalet above had been closed and shuttered since before she'd arrived at the beginning of May. And unfortunately Frau Wendl, the owner of the Pension, had gone down to Innsbruck for the day. Maybe she might try the Postamt?

Karen turned back towards the village. The sun was overhead now and she was hot and thirsty. Maybe in one of the bars there'd be a native who spoke good English. She took a short cut through the churchyard, the quickest way to the Gasthaus Himmelhof. No bird sang in the noonday heat. She turned her head to catch a glimpse of the towering pinnacle of the Wachstein and her feet came to a sudden halt.

She would have missed it altogether if she'd been looking straight ahead. Maybe it was the fact that the gravestone looked so new that drew her eyes. The inscription was in German but the name was the same. She had found Marisa.

* * *

The offices of the ski school were closed: the annexe had been transformed into a tourist information bureau. With a surge of thankfulness, Karen saw a familiar back as a hand chalked up a bus timetable on a slate outside the door. She had skied too often behind those broad shoulders to mistake them now. 'Franz!' she called out. A checked shirt in place of anorak, lederhosen instead of ski pants, but the smile was still there, the flash of white teeth in a deeply tanned face. He looked at her appreciatively.

184

'Noch schöner im Sommer!' he said. Once again, no interpreter was needed.

'And your husband?' he went on. Karen shook her head.

'Not here,' she said briefly. 'Listen, Franz, what happened to Marisa Weingartner?' His smile faded. Marisa had been popular in the village, admired for her near-national skiing status, liked for herself.

'It was . . . ein Unfall. You know?'

'Accident?' hazarded Karen.

'Accident. Yes. She did not have a chance. Another car came — and her Volkswagen, it fell off the road.' His gestures told the whole story. A car coming the other way down the mountain road, overtaking at a blind corner, smashing into Marisa: the Volkswagen knocked over the edge, spiralling down to destruction.

'Was she alone in the car?' asked Karen.

'Yes. She had been racing at Bad Gastein. She was coming home.'

'I am very sorry. She once stayed

185

with us in England. She came with a man called Tim Malone. Do you know him?' She reached into her handbag and showed him the picture she had managed to charm out of Tim's theatrical agency the day after she'd seen 'Flashback'. It was a copy of one of the stills outside the Serendipity Theatre. Tim was in profile, his arms around Philomena Johns. Franz studied the photograph with interest.

'He is an actor? Yes, he was staying at the chalet with Marisa. It was when she came back from St. Anton at Neujahr.' New Year. And January the second was the relevant date. 'It was meant to be secret,' said Franz. He grinned. 'But no-one has secrets in Dornberg.'

5

Tuesday, July the fifth was going to be another scorching day. Karen, who had returned the previous evening, woke early and went over to the window. By pressing against the frame and looking sidewards, you could just get a glimpse of the Thames. Barnscombe seemed like another life, The Salthouse the gingerbread house of fantasy. Reality was these four walls. Yet soon she would have to go back. The next step — the only one she could think of — would be an appointment with the family solicitor. Only a professional could advise her now. But there was no hurry. She wanted to visit Somerset House and check if Jenny had, inside the last year, requested a copy of the Will. She might also check on Judy Rycroft, Mark's ex-wife, just in case she should be able to throw any light on Jenny's state of mind just before she came to live at Barnscombe. And there was one question she particularly wanted to ask Tim Malone's theatrical agent. She'd very much like to know the terms of his contract.

As it turned out, she went back to Barnscombe as precipitately as she had departed, leaving the questions unanswered.

There was another letter from Mike on the hall table. Karen took it out with her into the summer morning and down Oakley Street to the embankment. The tide was high and the gulls were wheeling and if she closed her eyes she could imagine that the smell was the smell of Liffey water. 'I didn't mean to write again,' began Mike. 'At least, so I delude myself. But I have a piece of information that might interest you, irrelevant as it now seems. I went to Punchestown on Saturday and found that Malcolm McGill had a horse running. It didn't win but it was a good third so I went along to congratulate him. He didn't recognize me, which was important because otherwise he wouldn't have introduced the girl who was with him as he did. Eileen McGill, he said — Gavin's widow. When I responded with Michael Adair, the shutters came down with a clang. Pity. If I'd used another name, I might have got the chance of speaking to her alone. Not that I go for Irishwomen with black hair and sooty eyes. Not that I go for Irishwomen . . . I asked about George and was told he'd just won the East of Ireland golf championship. So somebody's happy. Let me know when you leave London. Take care. Mike.'

Karen had breakfast in a King's Road coffee bar. The roll was stale but the coffee was hot and strong. Afterwards, she wondered if she would have found a discarded newspaper in any other booth. Or would she have bought one that day? She doubted it. There wasn't much time for reading. Anyway, there was the *Mail* on the wooden seat and, because she wanted to get away from her own thoughts, she glanced through it as she sipped her coffee. The item was in the Stop press at the bottom of the last page and she missed it the first time around. It was when she'd re-folded the paper and pushed it away across the table that her eye picked up the word Barnscombe. Slowly she put her cup down. 'Death at Cobbler's Bay' was the caption. 'The body of a girl washed up this afternoon in Cobbler's Bay near Barnscombe in Devon was later identified as Jenny Hobson, aged twenty-three. Cause of death has not yet been determined.'

Part Three

1

Greg identified the body. He hadn't expected her to look so small.

*   *   *

The day Karen left Barnscombe, he'd left his house key at home because Tim had been using it the previous night. He wasn't worried when there was no answer to the doorbell. It was a fine evening and Karen might have gone swimming. He looked under the third flowerpot from the left outside the kitchen window and there, as expected, was Karen's key. He let himself into the hall.

Greg was not a particularly sensitive man but it seemed to him as he got the ice from the refrigerator, mixed a drink and took it into the sitting-room, that the house was an uninhabited shell. The kitchen was unnaturally tidy. And, come to think of it, the hall was bereft of Karen's usual cheerful clutter. Suppose she'd been taken ill . . . Suddenly alarmed, he hurried upstairs. When he went into their bedroom, he knew his first impression had been the right one. Two suitcases were missing from the top of the wardrobe.

There wasn't even a note. Surely she must have left a note. He ran downstairs again in case somehow he'd missed it. Then back to bedroom and bathroom in a vain attempt to gauge, by what she'd taken, how long she'd be away. Blue sprigged cotton suit, denim trouser suit, cream poplin dress, navy sweater, white raincoat . . . that lot could last for a week or a month. Anyway, she could always buy what she needed. Restlessly he went downstairs, poured another drink and left it untouched. Would she have gone to relatives — her aunt and uncle? Unlikely. Jenny? He flinched at the thought of Jenny. The twins? Ah, that was possible. At least she might be in touch with them. His hand reached out for the green leather book beside the telephone in the hall.

And yet . . . What was he to say? Karen had found out, that was all there was to it. She would come back eventually because the house was hers. But as far as she was concerned, he had forfeited any claim.

He stayed on at The Salthouse, partly because he had nowhere else to go and partly in the hope that one day the doorbell would ring and she would be there. To anyone who enquired, he said that her aunt in Sevenoaks had had an accident. Once, in the hours before dawn, he wondered if she'd gone away with Tim Malone. But no. Somehow he knew that if she'd left him with someone else, she would have told him. Sometimes he thought of the risks he had taken and knew that he would do it all again.

At the end of the first week, Mark asked how long Karen would be staying at Sevenoaks.

'Sevenoaks?' asked Greg blankly.

'With her aunt. The one who's had an accident.'

'Oh that! Another ten days or so, I think.'

'That should give you time to think up a more convincing story,' said Mark. Greg sat down abruptly on the chair behind his desk.

'Is it so obvious?'

'Only to me. And that's because you don't talk about her.' He took off his glasses and polished them with a corner of his handkerchief. He liked Greg. They'd always got on well together and, as far as business was concerned, they had an instinctive understanding. Yet often he felt that he didn't know Greg at all, that life in Canada had produced a man with a different set of values to the ones he knew. The thought of Karen brought with it a familiar feeling of apprehension. He had this absurd notion that she was in danger and that he had to devise a way of protecting her. Usually it was enough to know that she was there, that he could be in contact by lifting the receiver, see her once or twice a week. But now he didn't know what had happened and could find no valid reason for asking. His voice was sharper than he'd intended when he spoke.

'I've got Jenny's file here . . . '

Greg stood up and banged his fist on the desk.

'What the hell has Jenny got to do with it?' he shouted.

'I was going through her file.' Mark ignored the outburst. 'Usually, as you know, I leave all administrative details to you, but I wanted to verify a point in the contract. You didn't tell me that it was you who finally financed the novel.'

★   ★   ★

The days passed slowly, the nights were endless. Greg brought back files from the office to stupefy his mind with statistics. At the weekend, he played indifferent golf and drank in pubs where no one knew him. Looking back afterwards, he was amazed to discover that it was less than a fortnight from the morning Karen left to the morning Jenny's message arrived.

It was a typewritten note with Jenny's sprawling signature. He didn't think of looking at the postmark. He just crumpled paper and envelope and threw them into the wastepaper basket. It did occur to him that Jenny was being unnecessarily dramatic, but as he wasn't sleeping well anyway it would be no trouble to meet her at dawn.

★   ★   ★

It was still dark when he rolled out of bed, pulled on jeans and sweater and let himself out of the front door. There was a faint lightening in the east as he emerged on the cliff path and set off in the direction of Cobbler's Bay. The only sounds were the wash of the waves on the rocks below and the cry of a seabird somewhere ahead. As he walked it was with increasing determination that this time it would be different. This time there would be no ultimatums, no more demands. After this time, he was finished with Jenny.

2

Tim attended the funeral, even though it meant a dash back afterwards for the evening performance. He felt it was the least he could do.

★ ★ ★

Tim had never been attracted to Jenny but she served a useful purpose in bringing him back into Karen's life. At any rate, that was how it had looked at the time.

It was at a party in Hampstead — he'd forgotten whose or even why he'd been there — that Jenny had invited him, oh so casually, to Brighton. Chiefly because he had never forgiven Karen and, ironically, never been able to forget her, he went. That was an evening he remembered as if it were yesterday.

He had booked into the Ship for the night because one never knew when a session might end or privacy be essential. Then he walked up the hill to a pub called the Trafalgar. He didn't know till later that it was Karen's farewell to the theatre and that she was going to marry the tall dark man with the Canadian — was that what it was? — accent. But the moment he walked into the bar and saw the possessive arm round her shoulder and her smiling, happy acquiesence, he knew that he hated her. The room at the Ship turned out to be an unnecessary extravagance. After a couple of drinks at the Trafalgar, he collected his overnight bag and drove back to London. The only thing he retained was Jenny's phone number scribbled on a cigarette packet. Jenny liked him. Jenny was his only link with Karen and he had to keep in touch with Karen. He could never repudiate her as once she had rejected him. But there must be other ways of retaliation.

Over the next year he had spent

maybe half a dozen weekends at The Salthouse and kept Jenny attached in London by the simple method of neglecting her for weeks at a time. He never mentioned Jenny to Karen and he never gave Karen an inkling of how he felt towards her now. Except — except on one occasion. He'd been afraid then that she'd guessed. After all, she had once known him very well. But fortunately she had thought that it was Greg he disliked. Typical feminine vanity. After a year, patience was running out. The marriage, if tempestuous, showed no sign of disintegration. He could stand no more of a serene and complacent Karen. When Jenny came up with her scheme, he was committed from the first sentence.

'Would you describe yourself as an established family friend?' Jenny asked him one evening in the flat at Holland Park.

'If there's anything in it for me,' he answered lightly.

There was a subdued air of excitement about Jenny.

'And you could use some money?'

'Couldn't we all!' said Tim bitterly. Parts were hard to come by, especially after the spectacular failure of his first West End venture.

'And I'm right in thinking you wouldn't mind giving my sister a shove if she was standing at the edge of a precipice?'

'Unobserved, of course,' agreed Tim, willing to play along. He was slightly startled by this unexpected display of sisterly venom but he could always say later that he misunderstood.

'Then this could be the answer,' said Jenny and whipped a document out of her handbag. 'I've got to have money to get my book published. Once it's in print I know it'll be a best seller and from then on I'll be able to choose my publisher. But to start with, it'll have to be Carnlough Books.'

'Couldn't there be other ways of paying?' suggested Tim mildly. He could hardly wait to have a look at the piece of paper she was waving about. But it was no use trying to hurry Jenny. She took things in her own way or not at all.

'Of course!' she said contemptuously. 'On the whole I prefer cash. I suppose Mark might play,' she went on, 'but I don't see Greg preferring me to Karen, do you?'

'I rather go for that idea,' said Tim, momentarily diverted from the financial angle. Karen humiliated, discarded . . .

'Anyway, it won't be necessary,' Jenny put in impatiently. 'The other day I thought it might be worth having a look at my mother's Will. I'd never really studied it. In fact, I doubt if I'd ever seen it before because when they died I was still at school. Anyway, I went to Somerset House. Here's a copy.' She unfolded the document. 'And here . . . ' she pointed at an underlined section . . . 'is the bit that matters.'

Tim read the relevant lines in one swift glance.

'When do we start?' he asked.

*   *   *

Well, that was all water under the bridge. The first attempt, like all good plans, was the simplest. Jenny had worked out the tides and blocked the operative end of the channel, he had slipped Torhead Steps into the conversation. According to Karen's dramatic account, it had very nearly succeeded. She had only avoided a nasty battering by a split second's timing.

'What if she'd been drowned?' Tim had queried later.

'I'd get a lot more money,' said Jenny simply. 'But accidents are more difficult to prove than murder.' He remembered he'd looked at her with something like horror. Cold-blooded little monster. He knew, in his rare moments of honesty, that he was intolerant of criticism or the reverse but he would never have admitted to such dedicated animosity.

The second attempt had required opportunism, skill and a certain amount of luck. When Greg and Karen decided on a skiing holiday, it was predictable that they would choose Dornberg. It only remained for him to cash in. He'd flown over at the beginning of January and stayed with Marisa, telling her to keep it a secret. She was in love with him, hoping one day to marry him. Poor Marisa . . . The operation had been cleverly executed. It had only failed because Karen had shown unexpected presence of mind. Marisa was delighted when it all turned out to be a harmless prank, just like he'd said.

The third episode was Jenny's idea and she was the one who had botched it. Her inadvertent touch on the doorbell had brought Karen who was, unlike Greg, a light sleeper, out onto the landing too soon and too slowly. He and Jenny had returned from a midnight swim. The plan was for Jenny to let out a piercing scream in the dark hall and for him, in the confusion following Karen's fall, to remove the piece of wire which had tripped her. He had been bitterly angry at the time. But, driving back to London after that last weekend at The Salthouse, it burst on him like a revelation that out of defeat had come victory. Not monetary victory but glorious, uncalculated, satisfying revenge. No less than the breakup of Karen's marriage. Because surely she must have worked out for herself that the only person present at all three attempts on her life had been Greg.

As far as he was concerned, that was the end of the campaign. Even if he had still needed the money, it certainly wasn't worth the risk. At the thought of the risks already run, Tim felt a sudden cold prick of terror. Audiences are fickle: and while a rousing scandal could be good for publicity, he was uneasily aware that what he had done would be construed as a mean and sordid plot against a girl whose only crime had been her refusal to marry him. If even a hint came out, he would be finished in the theatre.

It didn't occur to him then that Jenny could be a real threat to a promising future.

★   ★   ★

It had been an exacting Sunday charity performance the night before Jenny's death, but Tim had no intention of going to bed. He mixed himself a drink in the living-room of his flat in Strand-on-the-Green and thought about Karen. He'd seen her one night, sitting in the stalls with Trevor Allen, but by the time he'd reached the street they had both disappeared. No sign of Greg . . . Could the marriage have broken up already?

Twenty minutes later, he drove out of the underground car park and accelerated towards the Chiswick fly-over.

3

Jenny fell like a stone. She didn't even see the gentle waves which enfolded her.

★   ★   ★

The day she saw her book in print and held it in her hands was the most important in Jenny's life. This was the first firm foothold on the ladder and she had achieved it entirely by her own efforts. The three-point plan evolved when first she heard about Carnlough Books — Karen to provide the background, Mark the literary approval and Greg the financial aid — had been, to her mind, a logical progression. Success had been the end result.

Getting Karen to invite her for an indefinite stay at The Salthouse had been child's play. Karen had accepted her sister had left 'Denim' and shed to have a base while looking ound for a more lucrative job. Lucrative was a good word, nearly as good as bonus. The bonus had been the discovery of the codicil concerning Karen's possible disablement. That and Tim's subsequent collaboration. Lucky she'd noticed that day at the Trafalgar how Tim had reacted when he took in the significance of Greg and Karen together. It could have been jealousy that had caused him to leave the party so soon, but Jenny had divined that he simply could not bear that someone else should succeed where he himself had failed. Yes, Karen had been easy. Karen hadn't even suspected that she was being used as collateral for eight hundred pounds.

Mark had been a different matter. Mark was the kingpin. His approval was essential to publication. Jenny knew she could write: so far no-one had been willing to take the chance that she would sell. Mark was going to be that man.

'What's he like?' she asked casually. She remembered it wa. after she'd come to Barnscombe. Sr. been standing at the kitchen tabr doing the helpful little sister act, chopping vegetables for a casserole.

'You mean professionally?' Karen asked dryly. Jenny kept her eyes on the onion she was slicing. Karen could be shrewd.

'No — I mean as a man. What does he look like? What's his scene? '

'Early thirties. Brown hair, receding a bit. Medium height, slim. Sense of humour. Was once married to someone called Judy.'

'What happened to Judy?' Jenny's voice held a nice blend of politeness and disinterest. As if she didn't know . . .

It hadn't been difficult to track Judy Rycroft to Reading University, where she was now doing a postgraduate course, and arrange an accidental meeting. Quite a few of the girls at 'Denim' had degrees: one had been

o shake the dust of Reading off
et not six months previously. Judy
been a surprise — something like
rself but pretty. The shape of the face
was similar, without Jenny's overlong
jaw, the eyes were a sparkling amber.
An attribute probably even more
attractive to the male was the delicate
air of withdrawal. Jenny practised it in
front of the mirror: it wasn't very
difficult, you just had to widen your
eyes and think of something far away.

'Mark never talks about her' said
Karen shortly. She hoped Jenny wasn't
going to upset the easy companionship
she and Greg had formed with Mark.

'Anyway,' she continued, 'you'll be
meeting him on Sunday. He's coming
to lunch.' Sunday. That was the day
Tim was coming, though Karen didn't
know it yet. That was the day of the
spring tide, and, with any luck, a
freshening wind. Would Mark's presence make any difference? Not really. In
fact, an extra voice would be an
advantage in blurring the issue in case

anyone got round to wondering who had mentioned Torhead Steps.

As it turned out, it had been unnecessary trying to make a physical impression on Mark. He reviewed the book on its merits and that was that. But when she tried to thank him ... She tried not to think about that particular episode.

★   ★   ★

Greg was the imponderable. It was Greg, in the end, who underlined the maxim about playing with fire.

At first he was just an adjunct, the typical brother-in-law. From veiled hostility, his manner settled into polite indifference. Jenny treated him warily, knowing that she was going to need his help, but unable to suppress the occasional snide remark or provocative gesture. Once her novel had been accepted by Carnlough Books, she cut down on the sarcasm and stepped up the provocation. The moment she had been waiting for came one hot day towards the end of August. Over breakfast, Greg mentioned that he'd probably be home early because of an unofficial half holiday. Karen said unconcernedly that she would be out most of the afternoon. Jenny added marmalade to the butter on her toast.

Shortly before three o'clock, the front door opened and shut again. Jenny, in the sitting-room, quickly stretched out on the sofa, long legs under short skirt, hair ruffled against a bright blue cushion. When Greg came in, she turned her head slowly and opened her eyes.

'I must have been asleep,' she said and swung her legs to the floor.

He was standing by the window. She followed him, barefoot. He half-turned as she came up beside him. The silence of the empty house was a third entity, impossible to ignore. She looked up at him. That was when the totally unexpected happened. For the first time in her narrow, scheming, self-absorbed life, Jenny fell in love.

All the moves she had so meticulously planned vanished like snow in April. Without conscious thought, her hands moved up and started to undo the buttons down the front of her green cotton dress.

*   *   *

It was the only time they made love. That, raged Jenny, as though she were the injured party, was Karen's fault. Her sister must have come back and seen them together. How else explain her eventual return, white-faced and shivering, long after tea-time? Summer flu, she had explained, and got through the dinner party by the aid of will-power and whisky. Greg appeared to believe it and fussed around with aspirin and advice. But thereafter he never, if he could avoid it, saw Jenny alone. There had been one brief moment, the time she told him about the baby, when he had really looked at her again. Then his face had gone blank and he said that even if he wished to leave Karen, he could not marry her. Jenny the realist, who saw no future in bringing up a child alone, had agreed to an abortion. Jenny, the girl who still hungered for his touch, had cried and clung to him. Jenny the opportunist demanded an immediate loan to finance the publication of her book.

*　　*　　*

Jenny arrived first at the rendezvous on the cliffs above Cobbler's Bay. Dawn on Monday, July the fifth, was still a promise in the sky when she parked the motor-scooter beside the path and leant against the fence. Her back was turned to the grey amorphous mass of the sea, but she sensed from the sound of the waves on the rocks below that the tide must be just on the ebb. Living at Margot's cottage the last couple of weeks she had absorbed its moods and changes, as she sat and wrote, without even looking out of the window. The

216

new book was going well. There was just that bit at the end of the fourth chapter . . . Jenny's hand went to the pocket of her skirt and brought out a packet of cigarettes. She swung round to shield the match from the offshore breeze and stood watching a band of light on the horizon shade into palest duck-egg blue.

She never heard the footsteps on the turf behind her. The wire strands of a fence which had always been more deterrent than safeguard sagged as one strong arm encircled her waist and another caught her just above her knees. She screamed only once, clawing frantically at the sun-scorched grass. Then her impetus carried her over the edge.

Unlike her egocentric hero, Jimbo Kilroy, Jenny Hobson had played and lost.

4

Mark wrote a brief letter of sympathy and pushed it through the letter-box of The Salthouse. He didn't ring the doorbell.

★   ★   ★

Mark enjoyed his job with Carnlough Books. Many of the manuscripts he received were ill-spelt and without syntax, others so carefully worded that any spark of originality was smothered under a blanket of verbiage. Again, there were subjects esoteric to the point of non-comprehension. But there was always another morning, another post-bag. One day, he was sure, he would open a folder and know that this was the one, the book to bring profit to the firm and fame to the writer. Above all, it would be the justification of hours and days and weeks of patient evaluation. Jennys' novel was not that book, but he foresaw that it would sell and not only to the young. There was an edge of callousness that made an effective contrast to the exuberance of the writing. When he finished reading it, he stuck the green Accepted tab on the outside of the folder and sent it over to Greg for costing.

That evening he happened to be in Barnscombe, so he decided to call and tell Jenny in person. After all, she'd been waiting for this moment for a long time. Greg and Karen had gone to the cinema and Jenny was alone. She offered him a drink which he refused. He'd always been slightly wary of Jenny, sensing an unknown quality. But he forgot his reserve as he told her what he thought of her book and why he had recommended it for publication. She stood quite still, her eyes glowing. When he'd finished speaking, she took a step forward.

'How can I ever thank you?'

'What, for giving an opinion? That's my job.' Mark smiled — totally unprepared for what was to come.

'You mean, unbiased?' Jenny's voice was incredulous. She started to laugh. 'You mean that all that playacting has been a waste of time?' Still he didn't understand. 'I thought I'd impress you by reminding you of your wife. Don't tell me you didn't notice!'

In a searing flash of anger, Mark realized how completely he had been fooled. Not professionally — that had nothing to do with it. But personally . . .

'How did you know?' He noted with detachment that the knuckles clenched on the back of the chair were white. Yet his tone must be one of mild enquiry because Jenny was still laughing.

'I went to see her, of course.'

Mark hadn't hit another human being since he was a small boy and provoked beyond bearing by his older brother. This time his hand came up instinctively and he slapped Jenny hard across the face. Then he turned and walked out of the house. He was halfway back to Honiton before he found the courage to acknowledge the source of his anger. That was when he knew he was still in love with Judy.

* * *

He hadn't been home twenty minutes when Jenny phoned to apologize. Over the line came an undercurrent of fear.

'It's alright,' he said dryly, 'it won't make any difference to the production of the book.' But it would be a long time before he would risk facing Jenny again.

That night he dreamt about Judy and awoke to a sense of aching loss. Moonlight flooded the room. He had met Judy on a moonlit college lawn. That delicate air of withdrawal had continued to fascinate long after they were married. In the bitterness of the break-up, he had accused her of using it as a sexual ploy but in his heart he knew it wasn't true. He had lost her because she genuinely believed in academic achievement and he had offered only the bonds of domesticity. When she left him he had missed her, at times painfully, but he had assured himself that they were incompatible — and eventually had come to believe it. Later he had been attracted to Karen's silvery serenity: yet his feeling for her, he now saw, was one of deep affection and concern. If he ever grew old with anyone, it would be Judy with the amber eyes and the questing mind.

⋆   ⋆   ⋆

On the day of the inquest, Mark sat in Greg's office to take incoming calls. Several of the girls were on holiday at this time of year, so he hardly noticed a film of dust on the filing cabinets or the unemptied wastepaper basket. The file marked Jenny Hobson was open on the desk in front of him, and he was looking for a note on sales figures he'd stuck into it some days earlier. Exasperated, he held the covers and shook out the papers. It still wasn't there. Suddenly he remembered that he'd brought the file in here not long ago to discuss details of the contract with Greg. He peered down at the waste-paper basket. Could it be . . . ?

He uncrumpled the note only because it was roughly the same size as the memo he was seeking. Having read it, he went on searching till he found the envelope.

Part Four

1

The front door of The Salthouse was open wide. The stone-floored hall was cool after the heat and dust of the day. Karen dropped her suitcases and looked around her. The floor was clean, the chairs stood primly side by side. There was a vase of roses and delphiniums, the flowers obviously dumped unceremoniously into the water, on the telephone table. Greg, in his own way, was welcoming her home.

The back door opened and closed again. He stood at the end of the passage.

'How about a drink?' he said.

After the first couple of hours, it was almost as if she'd never been away. Jenny was briefly and formally discussed. Greg said the inquest was scheduled for the following Thursday. Karen said she'd get in touch with her aunt and uncle about the funeral.

Later they ate bacon and eggs at the kitchen table. She told him about the conspiracy without mentioning that she had gone away because she had been afraid that he had been part of it. She talked about Austria and Marisa. She didn't mention Ireland. He talked of Mark and the business and the increasing sales of Jenny's book. He didn't mention Cobbler's Bay. When she went upstairs to unpack, Karen saw that Greg had made up the bed in his dressing-room. She was grateful for that.

She came downstairs again and made coffee for them both.

'You remember,' she asked him casually, 'that time you were going back to Canada before we got married?' She couldn't see his face. His voice, when he answered, was as unconcerned as hers.

'You mean the time I *went* back to Canada.'

'Yes, of course. Only — there was a

strike on at the time, wasn't there?'

He didn't ask her how she knew or where this was all leading. Because it was all so unimportant?

'Where did you go when you left me that day?'

'Swissair,' Greg replied promptly. 'Geneva, to be precise.' As though details were written on a blackboard, Karen could see the times of the flights to Switzerland that day in April 'seventy-three. Basle 13.45. Geneva 15.30.

'You must have had some time to wait,' she said.

'That's right.' Greg spooned sugar into his cup of coffee. 'What *is* all this, anyway?' He sounded half-intrigued, half-exasperated.

'Well, why didn't you tell me at the time? You must have known beforehand that there were no flights to Canada.'

'Yes, I knew — but I saw no point in making a thing of it. The strike could have ended at any minute.' Well, that was plausible enough. You couldn't fault the lad on that one, as Mike would have said.

'But why Switzerland?' she persisted.

'Why not? I had to go somewhere and there was as good a chance of flying to, say, Seattle, as from anywhere else in Europe. And that, in fact, is what happened.' He finished his coffee and held out his cup for more. Karen refilled it, half of her mind assured, the other half reflecting that proof would be hard, if not impossible, to find. Anyway, what did it matter now? 'It's all so long ago,' she said and left it at that.

The telephone rang several times and Greg answered it. It seemed extraordinary to Karen that no-one seemed to have realized she'd been away.

★　★　★

The Misses Anstruther had missed Karen Marshall very much. Particularly Miss Agnes, who had got used to seeing that bright head through her telescope most days of the week. Edith missed her because Agnes did, and Baby because Greg didn't come into the Tucker's Arms when his wife was away from home. And she was sure that if she could only get another good look at him, she'd remember of whom he reminded her. At one time she'd thought it was Sean Connery, who wasn't Irish at all but Scots, but that wasn't right either. Yet she was sure that it was something to do with Ireland. Maybe one of the newspapers sent from Nancy's uncle in Dublin which found their way into the house . . . Baby counted out the residue of the week's pocket money and decided that there was just enough for one small vodka.

Miss Agnes Anstruther had had one of her bad nights. Unable to sleep for more than short, troubled periods, she had hobbled painfully out of bed just before dawn and settled in a chair by the window. As the first pale glimmer appeared in the east, she swept her telescope round the horizon. One moment everything was grey, the next she could see as far as the cliffs of Cobbler's Bay. There was a man standing there. She couldn't see his face because he seemed to be looking down at the sea. Miss Agnes adjusted the lens. Old and arthritic she might be but there was nothing wrong with her eyesight, and the new lens which had been her last Christmas present from her sisters made a big difference to the focus. The man straightened up and turned, as if he had heard an unexpected sound. The telescope wobbled from his feet up to his chin. Then the hands which held it dropped away as the old lady collapsed in her chair and slid gently to the floor.

2

The local police had no difficulty in discovering where Jenny Hobson had been living for the two or three weeks preceding her death. But it took some time and a cable to the United States to establish that Margo Peters, the new Mrs Julius Hyams III, had given no authorization for the occupation of her cottage at Torbay. The decision to marry next day instead of next month had put all other thoughts out of her mind and she had forgotten even to return the key to the agent and instruct him to sell. Jenny had entered and set up house, without permission but equally without financial obligation. She had been wandering around for some months, doing temporary jobs in Devon and Cornwall, waiting for the publication of her book. By the time that happened, she had saved enough money to keep her in food while she wrote the next one.

★   ★   ★

The inquest was held on Thursday. The nearest coroner's court sat at Charminster, ten miles inland from Barnscombe and not far from Honiton, in a room which was part of the Victorian town hall. There was a dais for the coroner, a desk for the clerk of the court, hard chairs for the jury and grudging accommodation for the public. A golden summer day glowed beyond the narrow windows. The interior was dark and smelt of dust and humanity.

Greg, in his grey pin-stripe, and Karen, wearing a dark blue linen suit, sat side by side and hoped it would soon be over. Karen was resigned to a harrowing half-hour, nothing more. Greg was grimly determined to walk out of the court a free man.

The first witnesses were the young couple who had found the body. Pete and Taffy Wilson had been finishing a picnic lunch at the Torhead end of Cobbler's Bay and were keeping an eye on the tide so as to get safely round to Magdalene Sands before they were cut off. They didn't look more than seventeen, dressed identically in denim jeans and jackets, his dark brown hair frizzing to the shoulders, hers cut short round a small, neat head. The girl did the talking while the boy watched her.

'Must've been after half-past two,' she said, 'because Pete said the tide was full about four o'clock and it was coming in fast. I got up to rinse the cups and I thought at first it was his jacket floating on the waves because he's always putting it down and forgetting it, so I dashed in after it. Then I saw her, face downwards . . . so I called Pete.'

The boy nodded. She looked at him with loving pride. 'He doesn't talk much but he's bright. He put the body above high water mark and then he went off and phoned the police. They knew who she was.'

Police Constable Brewis had been born and bred in Barnscombe and had no higher ambition than to qualify for a pension which would enable him, eventually, to live there in retirement. He had seen it grow from a fishing village to a popular resort and thanked heaven that land configuration made further building improbable. Increased population could mean promotion and promotion led to away postings.

'I was on duty, sir, last Monday afternoon and, having received a call for help, proceeded with Doctor Hastings in the police launch to the corner of Cobbler's Bay immediately adjacent to Torhead Steps where we recovered the body of the young lady. I recognized her as the younger daughter of the late Brigadier Hobson.'

Jenny, in life, would have been surprised at the depth of his knowledge of her background and career. PC Brewis gleaned information as effort-lessly as his wife acquired trading stamps and he would have considered it dereliction of duty if he hadn't had a mental dossier on all the adult residents and a pretty good idea of what their teenaged sons and daughters were up to as well. He knew there'd been stories linking Jenny Hobson with her brother-in-law, Greg Marshall, but he also knew his place. He was there to answer the coroner's questions: private speculation was prohibited. The coroner nodded.

'What did you do then?' he asked.

'We returned to the police station. While Doctor Hastings made a further examination, I telephoned The Salthouse where Mrs Marshall, Miss Hobson's sister, lives.' The constable was aware that Karen Marshall was away from home but naturally one stuck to normal procedure. 'There was no answer. I then got through to Honiton and was able to speak to Mr Marshall. He agreed to come down and make formal identification.'

'One last question. Did you form any impression as to where Miss Hobson

237

had entered the water?'

'As a matter of fact, sir, when I got back to the station I remembered a report — it just came in that morning — of an abandoned moped found by the path at the top of the cliffs above Cobbler's Bay. The report also mentioned that one of the wooden posts in the fence had been uprooted, causing several strands of wire to sag towards the ground. The fence, sir,' he added impressively, 'is less than five feet from the edge, and the turf slopes steeply away on the far side.'

⋆　⋆　⋆

The coroner, Marcus Kennedy, was a mild-mannered man in his early fifties. His wife played both golf and bridge with skill and energy so he rarely saw her, even at weekends. Rumour had it that they communicated in notes left around the house. Marcus felt that it was an admirable arrangement. The spoken word played such a large part in his official life that he was more than happy with the monosyllabic exchanges that passed for conversation at home.

Greg found that he distrusted this unemphatic tone. But when he met the shrewd grey eyes opposite him, he realized that there was no lack of authority in this court. He gave his name and address and confirmed that the dead girl was his wife's sister, Jennifer Mary.

'Your wife was away from home, Mr Marshall,' asked the coroner.

'Yes.' Greg had decided beforehand not to elaborate: just to answer the questions, if possible truthfully.

'When did she return?'

'On Tuesday evening?'

'When did you last see your sister-in-law alive?'

'She stayed with us for a weekend in the middle of June,' replied Greg. He hoped the coroner wouldn't notice that, strictly speaking, he had not answered the question he had been asked. Marcus Kennedy, well-versed in the evasion of witnesses, judged it to be unimportant.

'You haven't communicated with her since then?'

Greg didn't hesitate. Jenny, not he, had done the communicating.

'No,' he said.

'Did you know where she was living? What we are trying to ascertain, Mr Marshall, is how she came to her death in Cobbler's Bay. Have you any information?'

'No,' said Greg again and felt an almost irresistable compulsion to qualify the negative. Such as ... 'She can't have been living very far away because ... ' He felt the sweat break out on his forehead as he saw the self-made trap into which he had so nearly fallen.

He would have been even more unhappy if he had known that the note fixing the rendezvous with Jenny had just been retrieved from the wastepaper basket in his office.

3

The next witness was Doctor Hastings, who was in partnership with his wife and acted as police surgeon. He and Marcus Kennedy had been at school together and had kept up an undemanding friendship over the years. He stated that in his opinion death had been caused by drowning and there was evidence that the deceased had entered the water from a considerable height, evidence consistent with the view that the cliffs above Cobbler's Bay had been the scene of the fall.

'Can you give us some idea as to the time of death?' asked the coroner.

'As it happens, I can give you a very good idea,' said Edward Hastings briskly. The accident rate in Barnscombe was not unduly high: the majority of victims were summer visitors who appeared to regard a warning notice as a challenge rather than a safeguard. But Doctor Hastings, in his own way, was an expert. 'According to my calculations, she died between three forty-five and four-ten on the morning of Monday, July the fifth.'

He permitted himself a gratified smile at the surprise on the faces of the audience. It was only in the dock that he was allowed to shine these days. His wife, socially more acceptable and technically brilliant, considered the limelight was her prerogative. Marcus Kennedy, who had questioned his friend so often before, led into the established routine.

'You are, I believe, keen on sailing, Doctor Hastings?'

'I am.'

'Then you are familiar with the currents around this stretch of the coast?'

'Yes.'

'Will you please tell the court how you established the time of death.'

From the post-mortem examination, Edward Hastings explained, he had come to the conclusion that the body had been in the water at least ten hours. It must have caught the ebbing tide, so as to be swept away from the seashore. However, water must still have been fairly high to have carried it as far as the channel beyond Torhead Steps.

'High tide was three thirty-seven on Monday morning. My estimation is that for the body to have drifted sufficiently for the strong westerly current to deposit it where it was discovered, it must have entered the water between the limits I stated and probably nearer four-ten than three forty-five.'

The coroner paused for a moment, glancing at his notes.

'You said earlier,' he went on, 'that there was evidence the deceased entered the water from a considerable height. Would you please enlarge on that?'

'Certainly. There was extensive bruising on head and shoulders commensurate with impact of water on the body.' He stopped. The bruising above the knees could also have been caused by impact — or by the fence. There was no proof of human agency. He decided not to confuse the issue.

Marcus Kennedy gave no indication of having noticed the abrupt stop.

'In your opinion, was she dead when she entered the water?' he asked.

'Probably either dead or unconscious. Death could have been caused by shock rather than impact. She knew she was going over the edge, you see. I found fragments of grass under her fingernails.'

There was no need this time for a dramatic pause. Most of his audience could visualize only too clearly the frantic scrabbling for a handhold, the terrified realization of the abyss below. Had she screamed as she went over? For one brief moment, a faint echo seemed to hang in the crowded courtroom. Then Doctor Hastings stepped down and the spell was broken. Karen opened her eyes. Greg slowly and carefully relaxed. The men and women on the benches waited for the coroner to resume.

4

Inspector Williams of the Charminster C.I.D. filled in the immediate background. He was precise and articulate and apparently devoid of imagination. The gist of his statement was that the abandoned moped had been traced to a Miss Margo Peters of Beach Cottage, Torbay. The agents, Trevelyan and Summer, had not seen or heard from Miss Peters since she had instructed them to let the cottage the winter before last. The Torbay police effected an entrance ('you mean broke in?' enquired the coroner) and found signs of occupation.

'There was food and milk in the refrigerator and a pile of foolscap on the table in the living-room. On the top page,' intoned the inspector, 'was written 'Tracy and Mo and Tim and Whoever' by Jenny Hobson.

Questioned by the coroner, he stolidly affirmed that no one in the vicinity of Beach Cottage had heard signs of departure in the early hours of Monday morning, and there was no known reason for Miss Hobson's presence above Cobbler's Bay at dawn. Except, he added unexpectedly, that you never knew with authors.

* * *

Marcus Kennedy was no fool. He had studied the case with his customary attention to detail and sensed that Doctor Hastings had reservations about the bruising — not serious reservations, just an unsubstantial doubt. He took a decision.

'Would Mrs Marshall please take the stand,' he requested.

Karen rose from her seat. Greg, beside her, stiffened in sudden awareness of danger. The public waited covertly for signs of emotion. An only sister, after all . . .

'Your sister,' began Mr Kennedy, 'was wearing a short denim skirt, a sweater and canvas shoes.' It was more a statement than a question. 'Tell me, Mrs Marshall, did she bruise easily?' Into the silence that followed came an almost tangible ripple of interest. This could be a loaded question. Karen, too, half realized what was behind it. She had a brief picture of Jenny, as a child, falling from a tree: she remembered scuffles at school, more recently bruises on the arms once covered by the sleeves of a green cotton dress.

'Yes,' she answered.

'Thank you,' said the coroner.

The jury returned a verdict of Accidental Death and added a rider that the local authority should consider repositioning and strengthening the fence on the headland above Cobbler's Bay.

★ ★ ★

If she had a tender skin, Marcus Kennedy reflected as he walked back to his car, it seemed a reasonable assumption that the bruising above the knees was caused by the wire strands of the fence. There was no evidence that another human being had been near her on the clifftop.

The only person who could have told him otherwise was lying in the intensive care unit of Barnscombe General Hospital.

5

The implication of the coroner's question had not been lost on Karen. As she drove away with Greg she forced herself, for the first time, to face the possibility that Jenny's death had not been the result of leaning incautiously against a rickety fence. The possibility that someone had used force, causing bruises which had not necessarily been made by impact. Presumably Mr Kennedy had satisfied himself that contact with the fence could have caused the marks. But Mr Kennedy did not have her specialised knowledge. Mr Kennedy did not know that Tim Malone had a very good motive for murder.

It was an ironic twist, she reflected later, that the three agents in her own so-called accidents had been the official causes of Jenny's death, the wire, the cliff and the sea.

* * *

Greg asked Karen to drop him off at Carnlough Books. There was no point, he said, in sitting around at home for the rest of the day — unless he could help her at all. Karen replied composedly that there was nothing he could do. She intended to sort out Jenny's possessions and she would rather do that on her own. She promised to come and pick him up at the usual time.

The shock for Greg was all the greater in that at last he had been able to relax his guard. The inquest had been more of an ordeal than he had expected, especially when Karen was called to the stand. But it was all over now. He was sitting in his own chair behind his own desk, looking forward to dealing in his usual incisive fashion with the work which had accumulated over the last three days. When Mark came in, he looked up impatiently, intent on the figures on the desk in front of him.

Greg handled the note as gingerly as

250

if it were a potential letter-bomb.

'Where did you find it?' he asked tonelessly.

'In your wastepaper basket.' Mark didn't explain that he'd been searching for a piece of paper he'd mislaid. If Greg couldn't take that much on trust, they had no business being partners, let alone friends.

'Is that the envelope?' asked Greg. 'I never really noticed it.' He looked incuriously at the postmark. Exeter, 2.45 p.m., 2 July. First class mail. That fitted in alright. He looked up again, alerted by Mark's unnatural stillness. 'Yes, I kept the appointment,' he said. There was no point in lying to Mark. Besides, someone might have seen him. 'But I was too late. Maybe my watch was slow. I waited for about five minutes. Then I decided she'd never meant to show up and I went home. Oh, I saw the moped but I'd no reason then to connect it with Jenny. As far as I was concerned, the fence could have been in that condition for months.'

He stopped, aware that he was talking too much.

'You didn't tell the coroner?'

'He didn't ask me.'

'Your information would have helped with the timing,' said Mark mildly.

'Oh, for God's sake, Mark, it would only have confused the issue! The verdict was accidental death and that's the end of it. Burn the damn note, will you, and forget the whole thing.'

*   *   *

His big mistake, Mark reflected that evening, was in assuming that Greg had told Karen all about it. And once he'd made that initial remark, it was too late to draw back.

Karen had spent the afternoon going through the possessions Jenny had left at Beach Cottage and which had been released after the inquest. Jenny had always travelled light: manuscript and typewriter were, to her, the essentials of living. The clothes she bought were in the fashion of the moment, inexpensive and expendable. Make-up was packed in an old handbag; birth certificate, cheque book and copies of references were in a plain envelope. There were no photographs, souvenirs or ornaments. Karen put the manuscript on one side and made a pile of the clothes suitable for charity. When she finished, she saw to her surprise that the afternoon had vanished. She rang Greg.

'I'm so sorry, I forgot to look at the clock. Do you think Mark would drive you home? Ask him to come in for a drink. I haven't seen him for ages.'

The telephone rang as Karen was pouring out whisky. Greg went to answer it.

'I was worried about you,' said Mark. 'Greg was evasive, which isn't like him at all. First of all he said you'd gone to Sevenoaks, then he forgot he'd said it. Just as he was able to forget the letter from Jenny. Not that it would have made any difference to the verdict . . . '

Karen, her attention diverted by Greg's

conversation with the Golf Club Secretary, put her glass down on the windowsill. Then she went across and closed the door into the hall.

'What letter from Jenny?'

When Greg came back into the room, Mark was finishing his drink. Karen was curled in an armchair near the window and they were discussing summer holidays.

6

Jenny was buried on Saturday morning in the churchyard of St. Mary Magdalene. The funeral was private. The only near relations drove straight back to Sevenoaks after the service. They felt they had done their duty by a niece they had never understood, and the less said about the whole sorry business the better. Tim accepted the invitation to lunch at The Salthouse before returning to London.

All the way down, he had thought about the previous night's performance. A night to remember, a personal triumph. For the first time, he literally became the man who was tiring of Philomena, attracted to Jan, the man who finally fell in love with Jan. For the first time Philomena Johns, shining star of London and Broadway, was out-played by her carefully chosen leading man. He was realist enough to know

255

that it had been sparked off by Jan's genuine response and that it would probably never happen again. There would be no appreciation in the newspapers because there hadn't been a critic in sight, but the audience had risen to him. A night he would never forget.

Looking at Karen, her personality dimmed by the occasion, her face shadowed by a broad-brimmed hat, he knew that she would never trouble him again. All he felt now was a tepid affection, the kind bestowed on distant cousins or assistant stage managers. There was no place now, in his world, for anyone but Jan Patric.

Lunch consisted of a cold buffet, eaten while wandering round the dining-room. Afterwards Greg, who had been noticeably reticent, went out to mow the lawn. Karen made coffee and brought it into the sitting-room. 'Tim!' she said abruptly, 'when did you last see Jenny?'

This was a question Tim had been

expecting ever since Jenny's death. Not that it was relevant, of course, especially after the verdict. Karen, no doubt, simply wanted to talk about her sister.

'Must have been that weekend about the middle of June,' he answered. That was safe enough, if not strictly true.

'You didn't know she was living in Torbay?'

'I knew she was in Devon. She phoned me from Exeter.' That *was* true. Nothing like letting the truth serve one's purpose, thought Tim, and reserving one's acting ability for the convincing lie. Exeter, wondered Karen, where had she heard . . . Of course, that was where the letter had been posted.

'But she wrote you a note, Tim, didn't she,' Karen persisted. For some inexplicable reason, she had this idea that Jenny had arranged for both Greg and Tim to meet her at dawn. Something to do with her book?

'I didn't get a note from Jenny,' said Tim with obvious sincerity.

Karen was getting desperate. She got up and lit a cigarette. From the corner of her eye she could see Greg grappling with the motor-mower just beyond the flower-beds. That glimpse gave her the sense of security she needed to ask Tim the next question. Because it was practically an accusation of murder.

'Where were you on Sunday night?' Reluctantly she had to concede that his readiness to answer was a point in his favour.

'With Jan Patric,' he said simply. 'She lives in Bray.'

* * *

When he had gone, she sat and considered the two lines of enquiry left open to her. Jenny's typewriter and Jenny's unfinished novel.

Part Five

1

Miss Agnes Anstruther returned to full consciousness on the day of the inquest, but four more days passed before she learnt of Jenny Hobson's death. Her sisters would have kept it from her indefinitely had it not been for an account of the funeral in the Barnscombe Bugle. As that ceremony had been private, the reporter had recorded only the names of the mourners and allowed his imagination full rein in describing the scene of the fatal accident. Phrases like 'Beloved Younger Daughter of Gallant War Hero' and 'Best-selling Authoress Tragically Cut Off in her Prime' flowed mellifluously across the page Miss Agnes was holding in her gnarled hands.

'We didn't want to remind you,' said Edith, hovering anxiously.

'Remind me of what?' demanded

261

Agnes. 'The girl didn't even turn up at our sherry party!'

'Well, it was the day . . . I mean, the morning it happened,' floundered Edith.

'The time you had your stroke,' said Baby Anstruther bluntly. The pubs had been open for almost a quarter of an hour and not even one little drinkie had passed her lips the whole long day.

'Oh, that!' said Miss Agnes and closed her eyes.

The next day she wheedled the youngest nurse into finding her the copy of the Bugle which reported, verbatim, the proceedings of the previous Thursday's inquest. Then she requested a sheet of writing paper and an envelope and, propped up by her pillows, started to compose a letter.

★ ★ ★

Chief Constable Sir Neville Montgomery was used to receiving eccentric letters. Articulate people with grievances in this part of the world wrote to him instead of to their M.P., whom they had never met, or to the Times, which they rarely read. Not that he saw more than a fraction of them himself. Detective Constable Morton, who had an Oxford degree, was responsible for all incoming mail and dealt with routine matters himself. This particular morning, he knocked on the door of the Chief Constable's office and went in. 'The usual batch, sir,' he said cheerfully, 'except for this one.' On the top of the pile, unopened, was an envelope addressed in faultless copperplate to The Chief Constable of Devon and Cornwall, Police Headquarters, Exeter. At the top lefthand corner was written Personal and Urgent.

Neville Montgomery recognized the name as soon as he saw the signature. He found that he could even put a face to the sender. The Misses Anstruther were of his late father's generation and he could remember being taken, protesting, to the house on the hill when he was a small boy. In those days one could register a protest but one still obeyed one's parents. The address, he saw, was the Barnscombe General Hospital. The letter began: 'We have not met since the funeral of your father many years ago but I hope that you have not forgotten me. I would like to see you as soon as possible on a matter concerning the death of Miss Jenny Hobson. If you would be kind enough to let me know when you intend to pay me a visit, I will arrange for Mrs Karen Marshall, the dead girl's sister, to be present.'

The Chief Constable sat for a few minutes, looking at the characteristic handwriting. He had been on holiday in the South of France when young Jenny died but he had skimmed through the press account of the inquest, chiefly because he had several times played golf with Brigadier Hobson and enjoyed his company. Then he reached for the telephone and asked to be put through to Mr Marcus Kennedy.

*　*　*

Karen was still undecided how much she should say when she arrived at the hospital. She knew the Chief Constable was going to be there. As an old friend of the family, Miss Agnes had stressed over the telephone — but there must be a new development in the drama of Jenny's death to justify the call in the first place. If, as she suspected, Tim had been implicated, she was willing to tell everything she knew. But if there was a full-scale enquiry, then Greg would be involved. And she still had the note she had taken from Mark so that she could test it on Jenny's typewriter, the note that Greg believed Mark had destroyed. She hadn't asked him about it because she believed that if he wanted to tell her, he would. Each step of the way back to what their marriage had been must be carefully tested, and invasion of privacy was the last thing either of them desired at the moment. Yet how could she warn him without revealing that she knew about the rendezvous at dawn — the meeting arranged by the

265

note which had been, beyond doubt, tapped out on Jenny's typewriter.

★   ★   ★

Weeks afterwards, the Chief Constable wondered if things would have turned out differently had he kept the investigation in his own hands. But rules of procedure were composed to be observed. Detective Inspector Williams of the Charminster C.I.D. had been in charge of the original inquiry. It would be up to Inspector Williams to decide what, if anything, should be done regarding Miss Anstruther's information.

2

Judy Rycroft had been more upset than she would admit by Jenny Hobson's visit to Reading. It was the purpose behind the so-called accidental meeting that troubled her. Jenny had dropped her name into the conversation, secure in the knowledge that it would mean nothing. But Jenny Hobson didn't know that Judy had three great-aunts in Barnscombe, all inured from birth to respect family ties. She didn't know that great-aunt Edith deemed it her duty to write to its surviving members once a year. Even Mark wasn't aware of the relationship, chiefly because their brief married life had been spent in London. Aunt Edith, however, refused to believe that divorce was legal and included him in news of local personalities. At first Judy hadn't paid much attention to those letters — apart from the boring necessity of replying to them — but over the last couple of years she found that unconsciously she had been waiting for news of Greg and Karen and Jenny. And Mark. When Jenny appeared, out of the blue, in the university canteen, Judy had no doubt at all that Mark was the ultimate target.

Judy had a logical mind and two things were immediately apparent to her. One was that Mark was still free. The other was that she must still mean something in his life if potential wife number two was taking such trouble to chat up wife number one. Another feeling, which had nothing at all to do with logic, was that she didn't like Jenny Hobson one little bit. The long vacation stretched ahead of her. There was Greece in September with Alan, a prospect which failed to enchant. For the immediate future — well, it was a long time since she'd had a holiday by the sea. If she didn't go to Greece, she could afford a fortnight at the

Magdalene Sands Hotel near Barn-scombe.

★ ★ ★

Jan Patric had been born Janet Patterson, the third daughter of a contentedly reactionary parson in a remote Cotswold village. She was always thankful that funds had run out by the time her two elder sisters were enlivening Cheltenham Ladies' College, and that she had been sent by a practical mother to live during term-time with an aunt in Guildford and attend a large comprehensive school with her cousin. Angela had determined to be an actress at the age of seven and she took Jan along with her. Talent and luck are an invaluable combination. Jan had both. While Angela was playing ingenue parts at Birmingham Rep, Jan was auditioning for the coveted rôle of Julie in 'Flashback.' She was then seventeen. Six months later she fell in love with Tim Malone.

She had been curious about Tim from the start. Although he must be nearly fifteen years older than she was, he had an ageless quality which made his playing in the earlier scenes so convincing. He seemed to have no family, few friends. He'd mentioned someone called Karen, and he had a photograph of a gorgeous Austrian who signed herself Marisa but that was all. Maybe it was the glamour of the loner which appealed to Jan, maybe the increasingly emotional involvement on-stage. Whatever it was, she suddenly found that her response at the beginning of Act III was delightfully natural. He realized it too. She had known from the feel of his hands on her shoulders. They caught fire from each other. That had been a magical performance, probably never to be repeated. But in private the glow still lingered.

Jan was a stranger to jealousy till Karen Marshall turned up in the auditorium one night. She had sensed Tim's momentary distraction and followed the direction of his eyes. There was a girl sitting beside Trevor Allen, a girl with ash-blonde hair and wide-set eyes. There'd been no trouble in finding out from Trevor who she was and where she lived. Had Tim been lying when he said Karen didn't mean anything to him now? Jan, completely out of her depth in this her first adult relationship, decided that nothing was worse than uncertainty. There was no Sunday performance so she was free from late Saturday night till roughly 7 p.m. on Monday. As usual, when there was time to spend with her father, she went down to Sherington Ash in Gloucestershire. But this time she worked out that Sherington was less than two hours' drive from a place called Barnscombe in Devon.

★   ★   ★

Unaware of the gathering storm, Karen was reading the opening chapters of 'Tracy and Mo and Tim and Whoever' for the third time. There still seemed to

271

be a remnant of the autobiographical because the flat Jenny described sounded very like the one in Holland Park, but — as she would probably have pointed out in the foreword — all the characters were fictitious. Tracy and Tim were just names she knew and bore no resemblance to Tracy Evans and Tim Malone. Mo was an African, and the last character in the title was whoever happened along at any given moment to share conversation, board and — usually — bed. There was one love scene more explicit than any in 'Only One Can Play'. Once again, Karen thought of the tranced face turned up to Greg's. She thrust the picture away. But concentration had been broken. If there was a clue to Jenny's death in the words she had dreamed up in the cottage by the beach, then she, Karen, had missed it. Maybe Mark, with his trained eye, might spot something significant. She picked up the manuscript and went out into the hall.

The doorbell rang once, tentatively. Then again, firmly.

3

A small room at an exorbitant price was all that Judy Rycroft could find in the middle of July at the Magdalene Sands Hotel. As she intended to use the bedroom only for sleeping, she booked it and was rewarded with a magnificent view from the attic window. Little waves creamed their way across golden sands that first afternoon and seagulls soared over Torhead Steps. Judy changed into a bikini, covered it with a jade towelling dress and stepped out into the sunlight.

After three days of sun and wind, she felt more alive than at any time since the break-up of her marriage. She had dived from the rocks at the bottom of Torhead Steps, sunbathed on Magdalene Sands, walked along the cliffs above Cobbler's Bay. She ate with appetite, slept like a child. Visions of the silent corridors and shadowed libraries of postgraduate research seemed like yellowing photographs in a dusty album.

On Saturday evening she went into the bar for a drink before dinner. The couple she had arranged to meet were standing by the french windows overlooking the terrace, talking to another man. They had already turned and waved to her before she saw that the other man was Mark.

★   ★   ★

The postman was young and diffident. He told Karen it was his first job and he handed her a parcel addressed to Greg and an envelope with an Irish stamp.

Mike's letter took up from where the preceding one had left off, as if the intervening weeks had never been. 'I ran into Eileen McGill in Grafton Street,' he wrote, 'and persuaded her to have a cup of coffee with me. She's a girl who knows her own mind. Old-fashioned — maybe anachronistic is a

274

better word — in that she doesn't approve of the pill, gin and tonic, divorce, racing on Sunday or the President of the Irish Republic. She told me that George took to the gay life of ceilidh or hooley after his golfing triumph and was last seen heading, according to him, for Philadelphia. After that, I went to Davy Byrne's for a whisky and what appeared to be a reunion of the Ballybunion jet set. I missed you. Mike'.

Karen carefully put the paper back into the envelope. A letter, she thought, one could show to one's husband any day. Maybe one day she'd be able to . . .

★ ★ ★

Jan spent a miserable Sunday in Barnscombe. She'd arrived home to find her two married sisters, with their young, at Sherington for the weekend. Injudicious mention of the sea resulted in a prolonged and unbearable picnic.

Her only achievement lay in finding the address in the local directory and locating The Salthouse. She determined to make an early start next morning, call and see Karen Marshall and drive straight back to London from there.

4

Inspector Williams believed in getting on with things. He could have done without extra work on his plate at the moment, especially as he was shortly due to go on leave, but one didn't argue with one's Chief Constable. On Thursday the fifteenth, Sir Neville had shown him the statements made by Miss Agnes Anstruther and Mrs Karen Marshall. On Friday he travelled to London to have a word with Mr Tim Malone.

Before entering the block of flats at Strand-on-the-Green, the Inspector had a look at the underground car park and spoke to an assistant at the nearest filling station. He had made an appointment for two o'clock and the hour struck as he knocked on the front door of Flat 10A. He was aware of a certain anticipation. His wife had been a fan of Tim Malone's ever since the television series, and he looked forward to telling her, with discretion, of his impressions. The first impression was that Mr Malone had changed very little since the days of his success as Simon Harvard: the second, that he looked a most unlikely villain. Still, actors, like authors, were unpredictable.

'As I said on the telephone,' he began, accepting a seat and a cigarette, 'this is a routine matter. All the late Miss Hobson's friends are being questioned. I believe you attended her funeral?'

'Yes, I did,' said Tim, 'but more for her sister's sake. Mrs Marshall and I are old friends.' Nice to be able to say that so convincingly. He wandered over to the window. 'I don't quite understand, Inspector — I was told the verdict at the inquest was accidental death.'

'That is so. But an eye-witness, till recently too ill to testify, has informed us that she saw a man on the clifftop at the relevant time.'

'You mean around dawn on Monday the fifth.'

'How did you know that, sir?'

'How do you think I knew?' asked Tim impatiently. 'From Mrs Marshall, of course.' Surely the man hadn't thought he was setting a trap? 'Really, Inspector, I can't think what this has to do with me. I didn't go down till the funeral.'

'You did, however, make at least one other journey to the West Country in the last fortnight — did you not, sir?'

Tim turned his blandest face towards Inspector Williams, but secretly he had to acknowledge that this was a blow. How on earth — oh of course, the filling station on the next corner . . . Well, better admit to something innocuous.

'I drove down to see a friend in Exeter on — let me see — must have been Friday the second.' Better be exact about the date too: no doubt the ferocious-looking frizzy-haired boy at the filling station had a mind like a computer. Anyway, Exeter was a safely anonymous sort of place.

'You motored back the same day?'

'Of course. I had an evening performance. I left after an early lunch.'

The Inspector didn't pursue the subject. The switch was abrupt but Tim was expecting it.

'How well did you know Miss Hobson?'

'As I said before,' he answered smoothly, 'Karen and Greg Marshall are old friends, particularly Karen. I met Jenny several times at their house in Barnscombe. And once or twice, casually, when she was working here in London. That's all.' His tone indicated that he'd felt obliged to look up the kid sister but really, such a bore . . . Thank heaven, he was thinking, he'd never written to Jenny. The only time he'd needed to get in touch with her, he'd put a message in the personal column of a prearranged newspaper — and even then he'd had the sense to sign it with the initial M which, to anyone inquisitive, could equally have stood for Mark or Marshall.

The Inspector got to his feet. 'Thank you for your time,' he said formally. His glance swept round the room and came to rest on a framed photograph on a desk between the two wide windows. The girl was tall and slim, deeply tanned, skis slung over one shoulder.

'You a skiing man? Manage to get away last season?'

Tim had time for only one thought — that Marisa couldn't give him away because Marisa was dead — before he answered that they'd been rehearsing before Christmas and the show opened in January.

* * *

Derek Williams was not an imaginative man but he was a shrewd and experienced officer. A trap had been set and the victim had duly fallen into it.

281

5

The show-down with all the suspects present was not a dénouement Inspector Williams had ever used before. He enjoyed reading about it in detective fiction but considered the method both over-rated and melodramatic. However, under the rather unusual circumstances, it seemed to him to be the most likely way of arriving at the truth. He arranged to meet Greg Marshall, Tim Malone and Mark Rycroft at The Salthouse at ten o'clock on the morning of Monday the nineteenth of July.

Monday morning was grey and still. The previous night, copper coloured clouds had amassed along the horizon, bringing an unfulfilled promise of rain. The lurking thunderstorm heightened the subtle atmosphere of tension as Inspector Williams and Sergeant Kellogg followed Karen into the sitting-room and closed the door behind them. Greg and Mark turned round from the window at the far end of the room. Tim stubbed out a cigarette and lit another. Karen sat down in a shadowy corner and waited for her cue.

Sergeant Kellogg withdrew into another corner with his notebook. Inspector Williams ran a hand through his thinning sandy hair and took the centre of the stage.

'You all know by now,' he began, 'that a man was seen on the cliffs above Cobbler's Bay shortly after the presumed time of Jenny Hobson's fall. Naturally, our enquiries should begin with those who were closest to her because the supposition must be that she was there to meet someone she knew. Coincidence is stretched too far in postulating that a stranger would have been loitering at that particular place at that particular time.' He paused and looked at Greg. 'Mr Marshall, I believe you have something to tell us.'

It was Mark who had eventually persuaded Greg to bring Jenny's note to the attention of the Chief Constable. Karen had stayed in the background. But after her meeting with Sir Neville Montgomery, she had told Mark that there would be an enquiry and suggested that information voluntarily given would at least put Greg one step ahead. Especially as the police were bound to find out about the letter . . .

Inspector Williams produced a piece of paper and an envelope.

'I understand you received this letter at your office on the morning of Saturday, July the third?'

'Yes.' Greg's face was pale but his voice was firm.

'Do you work every Saturday morning?'

'Yes.'

'You had no doubt as to the authenticity of the letter?'

'None. It was just the sort of

284

damn-fool thing Jenny would do.'

'You decided to keep the rendezvous?'

'I wasn't sleeping very well anyway.' Greg shrugged his shoulders. 'And, in the heatwave, it was the best time of the day.' He might have been having a cosy chat about the weather. The Inspector's tone hardened.

'At what time did you reach the rendezvous, Mr Marshall?' Greg hesitated.

'I presume you looked at your watch to see if you were on time?'

'Yes. It was ten past four.'

'Dawn that day was at two minutes past.'

'It wasn't a business appointment, Inspector!' exploded Greg.

'Was Miss Hobson there when you arrived?' rapped out the Inspector.

'No, she wasn't!' With an effort, Greg lowered his voice. 'I didn't see or hear another human being.' Was that entirely true? Hadn't he had a fleeting impression of footsteps on the rocky slope down to Magdalene Sands? He couldn't be sure. Maybe it had been the unknown witness. 'There was a moped beside the path,' he went on, 'but I had no reason to connect it with Jenny. I waited around for a bit. Then I went home. Dammit, man, would I have left the note lying around if I'd had anything to do with her death?'

★ ★ ★

Tim's interrogation began on a low note and worked its way up to a resounding climax.

'You'll be glad to hear, sir, that I've been able to find a witness to your presence in Exeter on Friday, the second of this month.' Tim said hollowly that he was delighted. 'By a process of deduction that I'll explain in a minute,' went on Inspector Williams, 'we were able to find a clerk at the main post office who recognized you as Simon Harvard. You see, someone posted a letter in Exeter between 11.45 (the previous collection) and 2.45 that day — the letter which

Gregory Marshall received by first post next morning. Could it be a coincidence that you were in Exeter the same day? I don't think so. I have a theory that Miss Hobson neither wrote nor posted that letter herself. It was typed on her machine, of that there's no doubt, and the signature could be hers. But it's significant that Mr Rycroft has found traces on a piece of her manuscript of the name Jenny written several times — as if someone had been practising her signature.' He paused for a moment. 'The clerk in the post office remembers the date because she happened to glance at the calendar when you asked her if the letter would be delivered in Honiton the following morning.'

Tim closed his eyes. There was little point in denying it. He remembered the girl because she had a pronounced squint and he'd thought she was looking at him when she must have been studying the calendar. He had called on Jenny with a cooked chicken and a bottle of wine — surprise, he'd said. After lunch she went back to the table by the window and he'd asked if he could use her typewriter for a revised list of cues in Act III. Jenny, who was always on cloud nine when she was writing, never turned her head. He practised her signature a few times on a piece of flimsy, scrounged an envelope and stuck the letter into his pocket. He said how about meeting him at dawn on Monday above Cobbler's Bay. Jenny nodded absent-mindedly — impromptu picnics and dawn meetings were all a part of this lovely new way of life — and he drove off towards Exeter.

He opened his eyes and produced a wry smile.

'A fair cop!' he said. 'But it was only a practical joke, you know. Something dreamed up after a bottle of wine. I suppose in a way it's my fault she died and for that I'm bitterly sorry.' He looked towards Karen as though begging for forgiveness. 'But that's all there was to it.'

6

Thunder rumbled in the distance. A bank of indigo cloud was building up on the landward side. The room was shadowy as a summer dusk. No one moved to turn on a light.

'On that point we differ,' said the Inspector stonily. As nice a piece of acting as he'd ever seen. 'I suggest that you yourself reached Cobbler's Bay just before dawn and concealed yourself. You took a chance that Miss Hobson would arrive on time — and she did. After the fall, you retreated to the car you'd probably parked at Magdalene Sands so as to run no risk of being seen by Mr Marshall. If the verdict was accidental death, you were alright. If not, a scapegoat had been provided, especially if he neglected to destroy the note. When I spoke to you in London, I asked if you had made recent journeys to Devon other than the day of the funeral. I expected you to tell me about the one you deemed the least damaging to yourself — and you did. What time did you leave London, Mr Malone, during the night of July 4–5 in order to reach Cobbler's Bay just before dawn?'

Tim's face bore the expression of one listening to an interesting, if not particularly relevant, theory.

'I suppose it could have happened that way,' he said politely, 'if I hadn't spent the night in Bray.' Inspector Williams turned his head slightly. Karen spoke up from the gloom.

'If you're implying you were with Jan Patric,' she said steadily,'. 'I'm afraid it isn't true.' She realized now how it was she'd been taken in when he'd told her about it on the day of the funeral: all the other questions he had answered with obvious truth, so when he had lied she had believed him. 'You see, Jan called in here earlier this morning and I asked her.'

That was the bitterest blow of all. To

have Jan brought into it was more tha[...]
he could bear. He sprang to his feet.

'Of course she denied it!' he cried passionately. 'Her father's a clergyman. He'd be terribly hurt if he knew.'

The Inspector had the last word. 'The time may come,' he said mildly, 'when she will have to make a statement on oath.'

★   ★   ★

Lightning flickered across the sky but still the storm did not break. Tim sat down and lit another cigarette. He avoided looking at Karen. Derek Williams studied his notes. Personally, he had no doubt that both men had been present on the cliff-top around about dawn that Monday morning and that one of them had caused the girl to fall to her death. Officially, he was aware that there was very little supporting evidence. 'If you're about to ask me,' he went on, still addressing Tim, 'why you should want to harm a girl

...io was a mere acquaintance, I can tell
ou. Not only did you know Jenny
Hobson much better than you've
admitted, there is reason to believe that
you entered into a conspiracy with her
to defraud her sister, Mrs Marshall, at a
time when your career was at a low ebb.
Now that you are successful, you no
longer need the money. Also, something
else has become increasingly important
to you. Reputation. And who could
destroy that enviable public image at
the lift of a receiver? Jenny Hobson. Oh
yes, there was a motive.'

Tim said nothing. He felt it would be
impolitic to point out the lack of proof.
Time enough to do that if action were
taken. He glanced across at Greg who
seemed to be getting off extremely lightly.

'You too, Mr Marshall,' continued
the Inspector inexorably, 'had a motive.
Or rather, two possible motives. One is
that it was you who conspired with
Miss Hobson; the other is the brief
affair you had with her. In either case,
she could have threatened blackmail.'

As he finished speaking, Karen slipped out of the room. There was a sound of voices, of halting footsteps on the stone-floored hall. The door opened slowly. Miss Agnes Anstruther stood there, supported by her youngest sister.

A flash of lightning lit up the interior. Thunder cracked overhead. Miss Agnes saw two men, roughly the same build, standing side by side. For a moment she closed her eyes, while the picture at the end of her telescope re-formed in her mind's eye.

'His scarf was knotted at his throat,' she said in a surprisingly strong voice, 'like . . . '

'Like Gary Cooper in High Noon?' suggested Baby Anstruther. It was a lucky simile. Miss Agnes had seen the revival on television only last winter.

'Exactly,' she agreed.

Greg never wore a scarf, knotted or otherwise. Tim's was pure silk, in a paisley design.

★ ★ ★

It was the look of quiet satisfaction on the Inspector's face that stiffened Tim's resolution. There was no proof, he reassured himself. Even Miss Antruther, it transpired, had seen only a man alone at the edge of the cliff. A man she had identified chiefly by his neckwear. No one but he knew that Jenny would never have let him marry Jan, simply because she couldn't have Greg. Had he been conditioned by his association with Jenny? Maybe. He had planned her death with the same ruthlessness as they had plotted against Karen.

'No proof, I'm afraid,' said the Chief Constable. He wondered briefly if a confession could have been obtained had the matter been handled differently. Probably not. 'Mr Malone may well wish in days to come that he had undergone the notoriety of a trial,' he added dryly. 'There is no defence against rumour.'

★　★　★

The storm rolled away, the sun came out again. Greg, jubilant and relaxed, opened the windows and breathed in the salty air. Karen, coming back into the room, studied the back of his dark head, the set of his shoulders. Volatile, often unpredictable but surely with a hard core of dependability? Everything had been cleared up, docketed, explained. They could start all over again. And yet . . .

'Gavin?' she said softly.

Even if she hadn't seen his eyes, she would have known by the way he swung round when she spoke. His reaction was something impossible either to simulate or deny — instinctive acknowledgement of identity.

Epilogue

'Gavin McGill!' said Karen. She still couldn't quite believe that sudden flash of intuition. 'Yes, I've been to Ireland. I followed your footsteps. Oh you may have gone to Canada later, but you flew to Dublin first.' He didn't challenge her. He stood in silence. In some undefinable way, he already looked more like a Gavin than a Greg.

'I suppose,' she went on, feeling her way, 'that you had two passports, the Canadian one you'd acquired and the Irish one you'd kept up over the years. When you were eighteen, your foster-father told you about your parentage, and you went back to Ireland to look up your relations. You met Eileen and married her. You came to England but Eileen didn't like it and went back to Ireland. Right? She doesn't believe in divorce, so you had to wait the

296

statutory five years for desertion. Only two of those had passed when you met me.' She stopped. 'Why didn't you tell me?'

'I was so afraid of losing you,' he said.

It was all over now but at least he owed her an explanation.

'I took a chance. I decided that Gavin McGill would disappear. So I flew to Dublin, as you said, and stayed at a pub near Baltray. I went to Castlepark to see my Aunt Margaret. I'd guessed by then what had happened to my inheritance, so I insisted on compensation. I also reminded her,' he said grimly, 'that I'd be in exile the rest of my days because of her.' He turned away. 'Then I left my clothes on the beach and swam round to Clogher Head where I'd got a dinghy rented in the name of Greg Marshall. A wig, dark glasses, clothes and papers . . . '

Two small pieces clicked neatly into place. So *that* was how he'd got the money for his share in Carnlough Books. And that was why Margaret still flinched at the sound of his name. Or had she never really believed in so convenient a disappearance?

'How did you know?' asked Gavin.

'I suddenly thought,' answered Karen, 'of the orderly way in which you'd disposed of your life.'

'What will you do?' she asked him before he left.

'Eventually,' he said, 'I'll probably go back to Canada.'

★　★　★

When he had gone Karen went out into the garden. The only emotion was one of sadness.

The sky had the rain-washed clarity of an Irish landscape. As clearly as if she stood on a Dublin quay, she saw Mike with his unremarkable face, his wide mouth, his blessed normality. Mike, protected by his heritage and an instinctive wit. Capable of passion and deep family feeling. Life could not be without promise while it held Michael Adair.

★ ★ ★

'You knew all the time,' said Karen three months later.

'Yes.' Mike held her hands. 'I'd made a note of the date Gavin was born. Then I checked with Canadian Passport Control. But I couldn't tell you. I had to leave you to find out for yourself.'

We do hope that you have enjoyed reading this large print book.

Did you know that all of our titles are available for purchase?

We publish a wide range of high quality large print books including:
Romances, Mysteries, Classics
General Fiction
Non Fiction and Westerns

Special interest titles available in large print are:
The Little Oxford Dictionary
Music Book, Song Book
Hymn Book, Service Book

Also available from us courtesy of Oxford University Press:
Young Readers' Dictionary
(large print edition)
Young Readers' Thesaurus
(large print edition)

For further information or a free brochure, please contact us at:
Ulverscroft Large Print Books Ltd.,
The Green, Bradgate Road, Anstey,
Leicester, LE7 7FU, England.
Tel: (00 44) **0116 236 4325**
Fax: (00 44) **0116 234 0205**

Other titles in the
Linford Romance Library:

A FAMILY AFFAIR

Mel Vincent

When Harriet Maxwell, a divorced headteacher, spends the summer with her family in Spain, she falls in love with Carlos Mendoza: a widower with four children. But Harriet faces a dilemma: Zoe, her teenaged daughter, also falls for Carlos; the forthcoming marriage announcement cannot be made. Her predicament gets complicated when a misunderstanding prompts Carlos to leave. As Harriet copes with various family problems, and bonds with his children, she fears she will never see Carlos again.

LOVE IS A NEW WORLD

Helen Sharp

When Elizabeth Carleton met Jake Bartlett, Rolfe Sumner's farm-hand, her life changed forever. Despite her thinking him handsome, he was still a hired man. But in sleepy Washington, Vermont, Elizabeth found herself loving him, agreeing to marry him and becoming the owner of Sumner farm. And when she discovered Jake's dark secret, she fought to win him back from the edge of habitual bleakness — and won. For Liz, the summer she met Jake was the summer that changed her forever.

3 1221 08158 1899

THE FAMILY AT MILL HOUSE

Bryony Dene

Anna, unhappy after breaking off her engagement to the charming Bruce Grayson, leaves the city to teach in a Wiltshire village. However, she faces new problems and tensions when she becomes involved with the family at Mill House: Guy Deering, an embittered widower, his bored sister and his difficult child, Peter. How did Bruce and Guy know one another? What was the mystery surrounding Helen Deering's death? When Anna finds the answers, she also finds love and happiness.

PLANTAGENET PRINCESS

Hilda Brookman Stanier

Elizabeth of York is a controversial figure. Did she or did she not love her Uncle Richard? What was the relationship between herself and Margaret Beaufort, her mother-in-law? How much affection did Henry VII have for the niece of the man whose throne he had usurped by right of conquest? This book attempts to answer these questions and gain an insight into the life of Elizabeth of York.